Adonis & Venus 3

A DC Love Story

The finale

By: Ty Leese Javeh

Text **Treasured** to **22828**

To subscribe to our Mailing List.

Interested in becoming a part of

the Treasured Publications

family?

Submit manuscripts to

Info@Treasuredpub.com

Acknowledgments

As always, I thank God first for all my blessings and for always guiding me. My publisher Treasure of Treasured Publications for believing in me. My wonderful support team, my sisters, Samantha, Sabrina, Ladonna, and Shanika. My daughter and granddaughter, Tilysha and Teliyah, for being the reason I push to achieve success. My niece and nephew, Ricky and Daria, for loving me no matter how crazy and silly I can be. My pen sisters, Ms. T Nicole, Reign, Khamesia, Taucita, and Authoress Nicole Dior for allowing me to bother you daily with ideas or read this to see if it sounds good. I still stayed in you guys' inbox and emails. We pulled each other through the tough times and I thank you for being there and for encouraging and believing that I could do this. Ashley, Kevin, Andrea, Sekenah, Tekelia and Keisha, thanks for encouraging me every time I doubt myself. For the readers, thank you so much for reading my work, and following me and supporting me as a new author.

A note from the Author

At times I didn't believe in myself, but I have a wonderful team of people that had enough belief in me to push me to find belief in myself. I admit, sometimes I still need a swift kick in the tail to remove my self-doubt. I appreciate the people that give me that kick. I'm still learning my craft and appreciate all those who have given me advice or helped me understand what I needed to do to build myself as an author. I thank everyone for putting up with my indecisiveness and confusion. My mind is constantly filled with a ton of thoughts and I'm always coming up with new ideas. Some work, some don't, but as long as I keep striving I feel that I will have success. I hope all of you continue to strive for what you want and never doubt your ability.

Check out my other books available on Amazon, and Barnes & Noble

Survivor of Love 1 and 2

Adonis & Venus 1, 2, and 3

Contact Ty Leese Javeh:

Facebook: tyleesejaveh

Twitter: @tyleesejaveh

Instagram: @tyleesejaveh

www.tyleesejaveh.webs.com

Synopsis

The kidnapping of Adonis and Venus's newborn daughter, Serene, drives a wedge in their relationship. While Venus masks her pain with anger, Adonis feels the need to hide his pain internally. Venus thinks the kidnapping has something to do with his street life and blames him. What she doesn't know is he blames himself as well. Venus realizes that lashing out on everybody is hurting the ones she loves, especially Adonis. As Adonis takes every measure to find their missing daughter, it seems like the kidnapper is always one step ahead of him.

Kay Kay struggled with the decision of whether to have her child or not. Finally, she made a choice and wants Loco to support her decision. Unsure of how Loco will react to her decision, she avoids him, until one day he shows up unexpectedly at her door, wanting answers. Loco loves her and supports whatever decision she makes, but a night of good fun could turn their lives around forever.

Harrison Maxwell Beandion, or Beans, usually stays behind the scene and does his work on his own, but the kidnapping of Serene brings him out of the dark shadows and into the light. There's a side to Beans that not even Adonis knows. He finds out that Beans is much more than a behind the scenes type of guy, and the only things that will bring his dark side out is messing with his family.

Alexia is seeking revenge on Adonis and Venus. She blames them for her miserable life. She calls for the aid of someone close to her to make sure she gets her revenge. She's out for blood and will stop at nothing until she sees Adonis and Venus dead.

Will Adonis and Venus's relationship survive this ultimate test of love and loyalty? Will they find their missing child or will it be too late? Will Kay Kay's choice about her pregnancy cause friction in her and Loco's relationship? Can Venus overcome her pain and anger, or is murder the answer? With her mind set on killing Adonis, will it be hard for Venus to get past the hate and find the love that she has for him? Find out the answers to these questions and more in Adonis and Venus: A DC Love Story, the finale.

Last Time in Adonis & Venus 2.......

Adonis

"Hi, I came to see my baby," I told the nurse that was on duty. I hadn't met this nurse before, so I introduced myself. "I'm sorry for being rude. I'm Adonis Thompson, and Serene Thompson is my daughter."

She walked over to me and shook my hand. "Nice to meet you. I'm Tekelia, the evening nurse, and Serene's mom already took the baby to her room," she informed me.

"Thank you, Tekelia." I rushed to the elevator, eager to hold my precious daughter in my arms.

I was standing on the elevator, wishing that it would hurry up. It stopped and the doors opened. I rushed out of the elevator and down the hall. When I got to Venus's room, she was lying in the bed looking half asleep.

"Where's Serene?" I asked confused.

"She's in the nursery," she replied.

"I just left the nursery and they said you brought the baby up here," I told her.

7

She sat up in bed with a frightened look on her face.

"Adonis, where's my baby?" she asked. I shrugged my shoulders.

"The nurse said you have her."

Venus pushed the call button.

"WE NEED A NURSE!" I yelled down the hallway.

The nurse came rushing in the room.

"Is everything ok?" she asked.

"Where's my baby? Did she go for any tests?" I asked.

"No. She was in the nursery a while ago, did you go there?" she asked, confused.

"I went there. The nurse said Venus came and got her and she's not here. Are you telling me that my baby is missing? Please tell me that's not what you're telling me." Fear and anger was rising in my body at the same time.

"Adonis."

"What are you telling me nurse?" I was tryna remain calm.

"Adonis."

"One minute, Venus," I blew her off.

"Nurse, don't make me get ugly in this fuckin' hospital. Where in the fuck is my baby?" I raged.

"ADONIS!" Venus shouted.

"WHAT!"

"My ID band is missing!"

Venus

I had to be dreaming. This just couldn't be happening to me. My most important job in this life as a mom is to protect my child. I'm not even out of the hospital yet, and I already failed. As Adonis continued his rage on security and the staff, my body went numb. The hot tears that spilled from my eyes were as if a fountain was turned on. The yelling and screaming in the room began to irritate the fuck out of me. Why in the hell are these muthafuckas talking about what they did and thought, when my fucking child was missing? They needed to have their asses in motion to find her. I knew what Adonis was capable of doing as far as the streets, but I didn't give a fuck about that. I was mommy, and that automatically put an 'S' on my chest as if I was superwoman herself. I wiped my tears and sat up on the side of my bed. Adonis's voice was booming throughout the entire maternity ward floor. In frustration, I yelled out to whoever was listening,

"Why the fuck are you all standing around talking? Run the goddamn tapes and find out who got my fucking baby!"

The determination mixed with anger and desperation in my tone alerted everyone in my room to look my way. Good, now that I have everyone's attention, I'll be able to make some sense out of this.

"You fuckers are standing around trying to point blame and clear your own asses from being sued, and I don't give a fuck about any of that shit you're spitting! My fucking child is missing! I suggest you take me up to the security room and find out who the fuck was bold enough to take my fucking child! I want to know now! I don't give a fuck about your policy and procedure, take me to the cameras now!"

As if common sense clicked into Adonis's head, he started agreeing with me and demanded to be taken to the security cameras. After the staff cautiously tried to bark protocol and procedure, the look that I held assured them that whatever it was they were thinking, wasn't going according to their initial plans.

The pain I endured bringing my child into this world compared nothing to the pain in my heart of hearing my child was missing. Thoughts of her innocent self in the hands of a monster, not knowing if she was safe or hurt, gave me the strength to get out of my hospital bed and go into auto pilot. I saw Adonis on his phone, with a vein popping out of his head and neck. I didn't care about what he was doing or trying to do, I only wanted these incompetent fools to take me to the security monitors. I put on my game face and sprang into action.

"Nurse, get these fuckin' IV's and shit off of me now! I want to go to the security room," I raged.

"Ms. Bowman, I'm sorry, but—" The officer started to say something, but Adonis stepped in his face, cutting him off.

"Didn't you hear what the fuck she said? We don't give a fuck about no fuckin' policies and procedures. Take us to the got damn tapes now, or I will tear this muthafuckin' hospital up." His fists were balled up as spit was flying out of his mouth.

I had to step in 'cause they were about to meet Adonis the street nigga, and the last thing I needed was him going to jail.

"Officer, do you have any children?" I asked as calmly as I could.

"Yes, Ms. Bowman, I do, but—" I cut him off.

"What if your child went missing the day he or she was born? Would you give two fucks about policies and procedures?" He looked back and forth between me and Adonis as if he was thinking.

"Nurse, please get her a wheelchair," he said in a low voice.

The nurse nodded her head then left to get me a wheelchair, as I thanked the guard.

The nurse came back in with the wheelchair and helped me get in. She hooked the IV bag on the top, then we left the room to go look at the security footage.

Adonis

My mind was spinning as we walked down the hallway to the security room. I couldn't stop thinking how lost my princess must feel being with someone unfamiliar. I imagined her screaming and crying out for her mother. People don't realize that a baby growing inside of their mother feels everything that she feels. They learn about their mother from the inside. Once they are born and their mother holds them in her arms for the first time, they feel a sense of security. They know who she is and feel safe, as well as loved. Whoever has my baby better hope the police find them before I do, 'cause they gonna die if I find them.

I was mad as hell as I paced back and forth in the small ass security office, anxiously waiting for the muthafuckin' security officer to scan through the footage for the nursery room. He was looking at the timeframe for every hour of the day. All I needed him to look at was the footage of the time my daughter went missing. I slammed my hands down on the desk in front of the officer, making the monitor shake.

"Hurry the fuck up! I don't give a shit 'bout nothing that went on during the day. All I care 'bout is what the fuck happened to my got damn daughter," I fumed.

"Sir, I understand, but I have to go through the footage by the timeframe. I assure you that I will be getting to the time your daughter went missing very soon. Please, just calm down," he explained, trying to keep me calm.

"DON'T FUCKIN' TELL ME TO CALM THE FUCK DOWN!" I shouted. "My child went missing from this hospital, the very one you fake ass security officers are supposed to be guarding. Now do your fuckin' job and find the got damn footage, or I will shut this muthafucka down myself," I raged.

"Adonis, let him do what the hell he has to do to get to the footage," Venus grimaced.

The way she sounded concerned me. I looked over at her. She was slouched down in the wheelchair breathing heavily, as a look of pain swept across her face.

"Ms. Bowman, you shouldn't be up and about so soon after having a baby. I can take you back to your room so you can lie down," the other officer said.

"I'm not going no fuckin' where until I see what happened to my child," Venus grunted then closed her eyes. She was taking short quick breaths.

"Baby, you should be resting. I can handle this," I spoke calmly.

"I'll rest when I'm dead. Now everybody shut the hell up so this man can get to the got damn footage." She laid her head on the back of the chair and exhaled deeply.

Not wanting to make her more upset than she already was, I turned my attention back to the monitors. The footage was fuzzy, making it hard for us to see clearly.

"Wait, rewind the tape," I commanded. The officer was finally at the footage showing my baby.

I saw the nurse, Tekelia, picking up my child and walking over to some bitch dressed in a hospital gown. She was standing with her back turned towards the camera so her face couldn't be seen. She had the same light brown curly hair as Venus. I can spot my lady out of any crowd, and that wasn't Venus. I wheeled Venus closer to get a better look at the monitor to see if she could recognize anyone.

"Who the fuck is this bitch?" she questioned, pointing at the nurse with a frown on her face.

"She's the evening nurse, Tekelia. This footage is during a shift change," the officer informed us.

"Well, I didn't meet her. Shouldn't a new nurse want to know who the parents are before just giving the child to some stranger?" she queried.

The nurse walked over to the lady in the gown and scanned her wrist band, then she scanned Serene's foot band. She passed my daughter to this bitch with a big ass smile on her face. I know she was doing her job, but that shit really pissed me off. I felt like she was happy that she was giving this woman my child. They had a brief exchange of words before the bitch holding my daughter turned to leave.

The camera caught a glimpse of the woman's face, but she covered the top of her head with her gown to block herself from the view of the camera.

To me, it seemed like she already knew the camera was there. She put her head down, tilting it slightly to the right as she hurried out of the room.

"Wait, go back and pause so we can see her face again," I instructed the officer.

He rewound the tape to the image of her face, then paused it. Me and Venus stared closely at the image. Confusion was written on our faces. Neither one of us could recognize the bitch. The officer tried to enhance the video, but we still couldn't recognize her.

"Fuck this shit," I said under my breath as I bolted out of the office.

I closed my eyes and pinched the bridge of my nose, trying to suppress the fury that was burning inside of me. I was ready to murder everybody in the hospital. I felt a slight touch on my forearm. I opened my eyes and made contact with Venus, who was giving me a death stare. She motioned for me to lean closer. I leaned down, putting my ear near her mouth so I could hear what she had to say.

"If I find out this shit has anything to do with your lifestyle, you won't have to worry about niggas coming for you, 'cause I'ma kill you my damn self," she whispered in my ear, then mushed my head away.

She signaled for the nurse to come and wheel her back to her room. I stayed behind to make a phone call. I waited until everybody was out of sight, then called the one person that I knew could get to the bottom of this shit.

"Beans, I need you," I said as soon as he answered the phone.

"What's going on?" he asked with a hint of concern in his tone.

"Someone took my baby girl," I blurted out. I couldn't stop the tears from falling once I started to tell him the situation.

"Adonis, whatever you need me to do, I'll do it," he asserted.

Because of the severity of the situation, Beans sounded as if he was alarmed. I knew he was down for whatever I wanted him to do.

"I need you to hack into the security camera, get all the footage, and find out who the hell the girl in the video is," I gave him my order.

"I'm on it. Give me a second to get to my work station," he said.

Beans's equipment was some high-tech government shit, so I knew he would be able to hack in the security system, get the footage, and enhance the video enough to get a clear picture of the kidnapper. I waited on the line while he hacked into the system.

"Ok, I'm in," he notified me.

I gave him the time, the description of the bitch, and the name of the nurse on duty.

"Ok, Adonis. I will find this bitch and deliver her to you myself," he stated.

I hit up Loco and let him know what was going on. He told me that he had to make a quick stop, then he would be on the way. I ended the call, then got on the elevator heading back to the room. Leaning my head back against the wall, I let out a sigh then ran my hand over my head. I really hoped this didn't have shit to do with something I did in the streets. One thing Lavelle drilled in my head is street life and home life stay separate, and my street life has already hit home a couple of times. Venus's attempted kidnapping, and then mother being shot, now this shit. I swear if I don't catch a break soon, I'ma go the hell off and kill some muthafuckas.

"This shit is so fuckin' crazy," I mumbled to myself.

The elevator pinged, alerting me that it had reached my floor. I took my time going into the room. Venus not fuckin' with me right now, and I had to prepare myself for whatever I had coming my way.

I walked in the room and chills ran down my spine, as her eyes pierced me like bullets through my chest. Every step that I took from the door to the chair at her bedside, I could feel her eyes ripping me apart piece by piece. Even with the nurse checking her vitals and blocking me from her gaze, temporarily giving me some relief from her hatred, I could still feel her eyes peering at me.

"Ok, Ms. Bowman, your vitals look good so far. I'll be in to check on you a little later." I watched the nurse quietly exit the room, giving me a small smile on the way out.

I smiled back silently, begging her to stay. Before I could say any words, the door closed and I was left alone with my pissed off fiancée.

"Adonis, they're calling the DC police. I suggest you get on that fuckin' phone and call whoever the fuck you need to and tell them to handle that shit, now," she said through clenched teeth. "Fuck the police, the streets gonna handle this shit. I want her to die slow. I don't give a fuck how much money you have to spend, find that bitch. You don't fuck with my child and stay breathing; bring that bitch to me." With that being said, she collapsed on her pillow and rubbed her temples.

I didn't say a word. I took my phone outta my pocket and called Officer Dumas so him and Whitman could do what the fuck they had to do to be the officers that took the call. Dumas told me that he would make sure that he received the call and that him and Whitman would be here shortly. As I was getting off the phone with Dumas, Kay Kay was coming in the room looking distraught.

Kay Kay

When I received the call from Venus telling me that Serene was missing, I was hoping she was playing some sick twisted ass joke on me. But the sadness and tension that filled the air of her hospital room let me know that this shit was real. Seeing the dark, gloomy look in her and Adonis's eyes was heartbreaking. I rushed over to her bedside, embracing her as tight as I could. I looked over at Adonis, sitting in the chair with his head hanging down covered by his hands.

"How you holding up, Adonis?" I asked.

He looked up at me as if he was silently asking me what type of silly ass question is that.

"How the fuck you think I'm holding up, Kay Kay?" he snapped.

Usually I would've cursed his ass out for being rude to me, but I'm gonna excuse it this time strictly because of the situation.

"Who the hell do you think you are, talkin' to her like you ain't got no got damn sense? Get off yo' fuckin' ass and find my daughter and—" Venus started goin' in on Adonis, but he cut her off.

"And you need to shut the hell up and stop actin' like this shit's my fault. You angry and hurt, well so the fuck am I. But I'm not taking my shit out on you, and I'm not gonna sit here and let yo' ass keep fuckin' talkin' to me like I'm some fuckin' fuck boy. My daughter is missing too, Venus, or did yo' simple ass forget that?" He jumped up from the chair and stormed outta the room.

I looked from Venus to the slowly closing door that an enraged Adonis left out of. Both of my friends were broken and trying to cut each other as deep as possible. I had no fucking clue that Venus blamed Adonis for lil' mama being taken. Absently, I placed my hand on my stomach. This is exactly why Loco doesn't want to bring a baby into this lifestyle, and I understood perfectly. I sat on the bed beside Venus and took her hands.

"Vee, talk to me. Why do you blame Adonis for this?" I asked.

She stared as if her eyes were saying that I should already know the answer to my own question.

"Because, Kay Kay, my gut is telling me that this is somebody's fucked up way of retaliating against him," she responded.

She was dead ass serious, and I could see how she felt that way. Adonis and Loco both live the type of lifestyle that can get innocent family members killed. That's something we both knew going into the relationship with them, and I don't think she should be treating him this way. I placed my arm around her neck and pulled her close.

"I'm sorry this happened to you, Venus, but right now you and Adonis should be comforting each other, not fighting." I was being honest.

"Whatever, Kay Kay." She waved her hand, disregarding what I said.

A shadow moved past the corner of my eye, catching my attention. I glanced towards the door. Adonis was standing in the hallway talking to two police officers, the security officer, and Loco. My heart instantly started pounding. I haven't laid eyes on my nigga in months, and I missed him so much. I had to take a step away from our relationship to figure out what I really wanted to do about the baby. I went to the doctors to get information about having an abortion as well as information about pregnancy.

After going over all the information carefully, I was finally able to make a decision. I had been procrastinating on telling Loco, but I know I would have to tell him soon. I just didn't know if he'd support my decision. He reached out to me constantly, but most of the time I rejected his calls. I know it's wrong, but my heart wouldn't be able to take it if he doesn't support me on this.

The door opened, and Loco walked in with his hands in his pockets, looking sexy as hell. He was wearing dark blue jeans, a white tee, and some butter Timbs. His dreads were loose and hanging past his shoulders. I loved when he let his dreads down.

His eyes were locked on mine as he made his way over to Venus's bedside. His shoulders were slumped and sorrow was written all over his face.

"I promise you we gon' find Serene and take care of this shit," he assured her, then embraced her tightly.

"Loco, you better hope so. Yo' ass is on the line too," she spoke into his shoulder.

Adonis charged in and grabbed his phone off of the arm of the chair, then started walking toward the door. Venus's eyes narrowed as they followed his every move.

"I hate you so much right now," she chided.

He looked back at her with pain in his eyes. He responded by walking out of the door.

"How you doing, Kay Kay?" Loco asked.

"I'm ok," I replied dryly.

We stared at each other for a second. I could tell he wanted to say something, but before he could say anything, Adonis cracked the door and called for him. As soon as they left, Venus burst into tears.

"I'm so fuckin' angry, Kay Kay, I could kill him," she cried out.

"Venus, you don't mean that. Look at him, he's hurting too; cut him some slack," I said, as I moved closer to console her.

"You cut Loco some fuckin' slack," she spat. "It's been months and you still won't talk to him. Tell me, what the fuck did he do so wrong? You knew he didn't want a child, and now you pissed the fuck off 'cause he didn't jump for joy when you told him you were pregnant. What type of backwards ass shit is that?" I don't know how she turned this shit on me, but I'm not Adonis. She ain't taking her anger and frustration out on me.

"Look, Venus, I understand you hurting right now, and you pissed the hell off. But you ain't gonna turn that shit on me. I have my own reasons for not talking to him. Instead of going off on everybody, you need to stop and think about how you hurting the man you love. Look at him, he is as fucked up about this as you are."

"I don't give a fuck. I'm the one who carried my baby. I got to hold her one time, ONE TIME, Kay Kay, and now she's gone. How the fuck am I supposed to feel? And as for him being hurt, his ass

31

deserves to hurt. Look how many times he's hurt me, so fuck him and his fuckin' feelings. And if you feeling some type of way, I don't give a flying fuck. All I care about right now is my daughter being all alone with a stranger who could be doing God knows what to her. Understand that," she lashed out.

Her breathing became rapid as tears filled her eyes. She looked wide eyed as her eyes darted around the room as if she came to a realization.

"Kay Kay, my child is missing," she cried out as she covered her face with her hand and broke down crying uncontrollably.

She clenched her chest and started taking quick wheezing breaths as if she couldn't catch her breath. I screamed for a nurse. Adonis came rushing over to her bedside.

"Breathe, baby," he pleaded as he held her in his arms.

A nurse came rushing in the room telling us to move back. Me and Adonis quickly stepped away as the nurse tended to Venus. Adonis stood there with his hands on his head and fear was written all over his face.

"She's gonna be ok, Adonis." I gently rubbed his back, trying to comfort him.

Once the nurse stabilized Venus, she informed us that she had an anxiety attack and needed to rest. I grabbed my purse and gave her a kiss on the cheek.

"I'll come back tomorrow, ok?" I told her as she laid back on the pillow.

"Sit with her for a minute, Kay Kay, while I handle some shit really quick," Adonis said before leaving the room and joining the others in the hallway.

As Adonis was speaking to the gentlemen, I noticed Loco looking back and forth from Adonis to the room, staring only at me. I kept turning away, but every time I looked up, his eyes met mine and it felt like they were piercing through my body.

"Kay Kay, why don't you just talk to him?" Venus's voice slurred as she asked that question.

"I am. I just need to put my big girl panties on and do what I have to do," I replied.

She placed her hand on my arm.

"You know I'm sorry, right?" she blinked slowly.

"Yeah, I know. You going through a tough time. If I was you, I would probably be cussing everybody out too," I smiled at her.

She looked drunk and could hardly keep her eyes open.

"Venus, don't talk. Just close your eyes and go to sleep, and think about what I said. Adonis is hurting too," I advised.

She gave me a half smile as her eyes slowly closed.

I moved from the side of her bed to the chair, waiting for Adonis to come back in the room. I took out my phone and started browsing through a few things on the internet. I was sitting in the chair by her bedside with my legs crossed, bouncing my leg. I could feel Loco's eyes on me. I looked up and we made eye contact. It was over. Those eyes had me intrigued.

Loco

As Adonis was explaining what he needed from me, Dumas, and Whitman, I couldn't take my eyes off of Kay Kay. This was the first time I saw her in months. I wanted to talk to her to find out what was going on in our relationship. I was trying to give her time and space to figure out what she wanted, but fuck it, I can't do it anymore. I love and miss the shit outta her. I don't care how many times she said that we weren't broken up, her distance made me feel like that's exactly what it was. I was fucked up in the head, and that shit wasn't me. I needed her to understand that I gave her a part of me that no other woman but my mother has ever had—my fuckin' heart—and not being with her is killing me.

Every time I peeked in the room, I saw her sexy ass eyes staring back at me. My lips were begging to kiss those soft, juicy lips of hers. I needed to see them muthafuckas wrapped around my dick again. I swear ain't nothing better than looking down and seeing that shit. Fuck! I missed her ass. I even missed the way she hollered when I long stroked her ass. After all this time, she still screamed when I went deep. I felt my dick starting to brick up just thinking 'bout her sexy ass. I peeked in the room one more time. She was sitting in the chair, looking down at her phone, with her legs crossed bouncing it up and down. She stopped bouncing her leg and adjusted the string on the bottom of her pants. *Damn she look sexy as fuck,* I thought. She looked up from her phone and our eyes met. It seemed as if she was watching me just as much as I was watching her. I blew her a kiss and she smiled and turned her attention back to her phone.

A few minutes later, she stood up and stretched. Her shirt lifted up more, revealing her entire stomach. I slowly licked my lips. One thing I loved about Kay Kay is she stayed fresh. She was wearing a pair of denim joggers and a white cropped fitted tee, and a pair of sexy ass red bottoms. She looked towards the door and noticed me staring at her, licking my lips. She mouthed the word 'creep', as she folded her arms, pouting at me. I could see she was amused by the attention I was giving her 'cause she was blushing under her pouty face. I snickered.

"Muthafucka, are you paying attention to what the fuck I'm saying?" Adonis barked.

"Yeah, nigga, I heard every fuckin' word you said," I barked back.

"I can't tell the way you all in Kay Kay's fuckin' face. Nigga, deal with her on yo' own fuckin' time. I called you here for me and my needs, my nigga," he stated.

"Muthafucka, it's always about you and yo' needs. Do you ever just for one little second think about what the fuck other people need? Do you really fuckin' understand that the world doesn't revolve around YOU and what the fuck you want and need? Selfish ass nigga."

I know my nigga is going through some real serious shit right now, and I'm here to do whatever the fuck he needs me to do. But I swear, if it ain't about him, he doesn't give a shit about nothing. I have shit going on too. I spent all fuckin' day taking care of my moms, running her errands, making sure all her shit is done. The moment I thought I could go home and relax, this nigga calls and here I am right by his side, as always. He knows that I don't need to hear all this shit he talking. Just tell me who the fuck I need to kill and it's done.

"For real, nigga, you gon' talk shit while I'm going through this fucked up ass bullshit? You think I'm worried 'bout what the fuck you saying my dude? I don't give a fuck right now, real fucking talk." He walked up on me like he was about to jump and I didn't give a shit if he did. I wasn't about to back down.

"Nigga, you know me. I'll call you on your bullshit whenever the fuck I feel like it, no matter what the fuck is going on." I stepped closer to him. If shit was gon' go down, so be it.

"Y'all stop this bullshit right now. I don't know what the hell is going on and I don't give a fuck. Venus is in that room with a broken heart, suffering tremendously, and y'all two stupid muthafuckas out here tryna prove who got the biggest dick," Kay Kay snapped, getting our attention.

She was standing in the doorway with her hand on her hip and a mean ass mug on her face. She looked at Dumas and Whitman.

"And y'all two niggas should be ashamed to call y'all selves cops. Standing out here with dumb ass looks on your faces, watching these two knuckleheads go at it like lil' ass boys. Get y'all shit together or get the fuck out, and I'm talkin' to all four of y'all immature assholes." She cut her eyes at all of us, then turned on her heels and went back in the room.

Me and Adonis looked at each other and started cracking the fuck up.

"That's yo' girl," he chuckled.

"I know." I shook my head. "My bad, my nigga," I apologized, and gave him a brotherly hug. "But you still a selfish ass nigga," I continued.

"I know," he admitted.

He shook his head and let out a deep breath.

"Venus had her foot in my ass all day and I'm fuckin' drained," he expressed.

My nigga was stressed the fuck out.

"Ok, you two, get the fuck outta here. I'll call you later," he told Dumas and Whitman.

He looked at me and said, "I'm gon' go try to get some rest while she knocked out, 'cause I know I'ma hear her mouth as soon as she wakes up."

He turned to go inside the room.

"Adonis," I called. He looked back at me. "We gon' find Serene and bring her home safe," I assured him.

He nodded his head then went into the room. I walked down the hallway thinking about Kay Kay. Today made me truly understand why she wanted to abort the baby. It wasn't me. It was the same reason why I didn't want a child yet: my lifestyle.

After seeing what my man's going through, I supported her 100 percent. It was time for us to put all this stuff behind us and work this shit out. I don't know how, but I have to talk to her. I waited in the parking lot for Kay Kay to come out.

"Kay Kay," I called as she walked right past me.

She turned around with her arms folded across her chest.

"Can we talk?" I asked.

"Loco, for real, I'm too exhausted to deal with our problems right now," she replied.

"What problems, Kay Kay? I don't understand. You told me you were pregnant and I admit I—" I started to explain what I was feeling.

"LOCO!" she shouted, cutting me off. "Not tonight. I'm exhausted." She turned on her heels and stormed away.

"Aight, you wanna play hard. Fuck that shit, you gon' talk to me." I was talking to myself.

I looked up and this couple was staring at me like I was crazy.

"Fuck y'all looking at?" I questioned with a mug on my face.

I watched Kay Kay pull out of the parking lot, then I made my way to the car.

This shit ain't over, I thought, as I put the key in the ignition and started my car. I sat back thinking on how I could get Kay Kay to talk to me. I needed to let her know that I have her back no matter what. I decided to give her a few more days, but I had no intentions on letting Kay Kay go like that. There's one thing I could do to make sure Kay Kay had no choice but to talk this shit out. I pulled out of the parking lot and took my ass home. Shit, I was exhausted too.

Anonymous...

This damn baby has been crying since I got her, I thought, as I stumbled my way over to her crib. I guess she misses her fuckin' mother. I took a deep breath.

"Awww, don't cry, lil' momma. I'm gon' take good care of you," I said in a sweet pleasant voice as I picked Serene up and cradled her in my arms.

I bounced her slowly as I went in the kitchen to fix her a bottle.

"I have to find a way to make you forget all about yo' bitch of a mother. I hate her. You know that, pumpkin?" I sat in the chair and placed the bottle in her mouth. She started drinking like she was starving.

"You a greedy lil thing, aren't you?" I giggled, stroking her cheek as I watched her suck down that bottle.

"I know you're scared 'cause you don't know me yet. You want Venus, I know, but fuck her. I promise I'm gonna be a way better mommy to you than she would've ever been," I promised, as she finished the bottle.

I snuggled her against my shoulder and gently patted her back to burp her. She was squirming like a little worm. I giggled at the way she tensed her body, calling herself stretching. A few minutes later, she let out the cutest little milk smelling burp.

"See now, Serene, wasn't that quick and easy?" I spoke in a soft spoken voice as I laid her on the bed to change her.

She started wiggling around, making cute little faces, then she stuck her little tongue out.

"Awww, aren't you the cutest lil' thing." I tapped her tiny little nose with the tip of my finger.

I grabbed the rubbing alcohol and Q-tip to clean her belly button.

"I can't wait 'til this thing falls off." I scrunched my face in disgust. I hated how that shit looked.

After changing her diaper, I swaddled her in her blanket, sat in the chair and rocked her slowly.

"Hush little baby, don't you cry, mommy and daddy is gonna die. Don't worry, baby, I'ma call my goons, and I will be your mommy soon," I sang, rocking her to sleep.

"My beautiful Serene." I gently rubbed her head. "I have to remember to change your name," I whispered. I continued rocking her and singing my song, thinking of other names for her.

"Maurina. No... Macie. No... Maxie," I said to myself. I was tryna figure out a name to honor Maurice.

Serene drifted off to sleep. I slowly placed my precious new baby in her crib. She wiggled around and stretched, making little grunting noises. I gently stroked her back until she was comfortable and settled. I made sure her monitor was turned on, then went to the living room and flopped down on the couch.

"Damn, having a baby is more work than I thought," I said to myself, grabbing my glass of wine off the coffee table.

I needed to find a way to make some fast money. I had to get the hell away from here before I was found. I sat back against the couch, drinking my wine, and trying my best to figure shit out. Getting rid of Adonis and Venus was gonna take a lot of money and careful planning, especially if I was gonna raise their child as my own.

"I guess I have to turn to the world's oldest profession," I mumbled, as I thought of prostituting myself.

It's degrading, it disgusted me, but it was easy money. After deciding that prostitution was the only way for me, I finished off my glass and headed into the bedroom so I could get some sleep before my daughter woke up.

Beans

When Adonis called me and told me that his child was missing, I sprang into action. Over the years, Adonis had become like family to me. He's like that annoying ass nephew that's always fuckin' with you, but you can't help but to love him.

"Who are you?" I mumbled to myself, staring at the grainy footage.

I pulled up my system and typed in Harrison Maxwell Beandion; it always brought a smile to my face. Even after all these years, no one, including Adonis, knew my real name. I enhanced the image of the woman in the hospital gown as much as I could.

Okay, let's see who you are, I thought, as I scanned her image into the system. Being a Technical Surveillance Counter Measurement Specialist in the U.S. Marine Corps had its perks. I learned various techniques to prevent people from doing exactly what I was doing in that moment, hacking into computer systems. The image was too distorted for the program to work properly. I had to try other measurements. I pressed rewind on the video and watched it over again.

Rubbing my tired eyes, I leaned back in the chair, folding my arms across my chest. I glanced at the clock and realized I was staring at the computer screen for an hour.

"Shit, gimme something," I whispered as I stretched. Something caught my attention. There was a quick flash of something in the reflection of the nurse's eyes. I hit rewind, then played the tape again.

"I got you," I said to myself as I paused the tape and zoomed in.

"You two are good, but not good enough," I snickered.

As the nurse passed the woman the baby, the woman passed her a key. It was apparent to me these women were working together.

"Ok, ladies, it's time for me to find out how well you know each other," I said, as I hacked in to the hospital's personnel file.

Adonis gave me the name of the nurse on duty. I searched the database and got her name, address, and phone number. I jotted the information down on a piece of paper.

Aside from being trained in surveillance and military warfare, I retired from the CIA as an Intelligence Analyst. The only thing that could bring me out of retirement is fuckin' with family. Usually, I liked to stay behind the scenes and not get my hands dirty, but this time it's personal.

"You fucked with the wrong family, Ms. Tekelia Saunders," I said, as I snatched the paper off the desk and headed out the door.

2 days later

Venus

"This shit is so fuckin' ridiculous," I stated, shaking my knee from side to side, watching the clock as it changed from 11: 26 to 11:27 am. "How got damn long do to it take to discharge a person?" I huffed.

My mother was hastily running around the room gathering my stuff, irritating the fuck outta me. I watched her go back and forth, folding and putting things in bags.

"CAN YOU JUST SIT THE HELL DOWN!" I shouted, laying my head back against the pillow and rubbing my hand across my forehead, feeling annoyed.

"Venus, just try to calm down," my mother suggested, continuing to pack my stuff.

"CALM DOWN? CALM DOWN?" I yelled. I folded one arm across my midsection and pinched the bridge of my nose. I closed my eyes and took a breath. "How am I supposed to be calm? I'm leaving the hospital today without my child. Do you know how that feels?" I asked.

"No, Venus, I don't," she barked, slamming the bag on the bed. "But I do know about pain, anger, and loss." She walked around the bed and sat beside me. "I know you're hurt and mad as hell; I would be too. But you can't keep lashing out on everybody," she added.

"Oh, like you lashed out on me when I fucked perverted ass Willy for your crack?" I asked, giving her a vengeful look.

She tried to ignore the comment, but I could tell it penetrated her like a knife to the heart, cutting her deep.

"You don't have to remind me of the pain I caused you. I know I was a terrible mother. I know that." She reached for my hand and I pulled away. "I thought we moved past all that stuff." Her voice was brittle as she spoke. I felt horrible for bringing that up.

"You the same as me, Venus. I used drugs to mask my pain and you use anger. Either way it's wrong." She looked at me with tears in her eyes. "I hope you never understand my pain. There's a reason why you don't know who your father is."

She got up and walked out of the room. The way she held her head down and wrapped her arms around her trembling body as she left, let me know that I had taken her mind back to a place that she never wanted to visit. I closed my eyes tightly to hold back my tears.

I laid my head back as her words ran through my mind over and over again. I wanted to know what she meant by she hoped I never understood her pain, and what does that have to do with my father? I twirled my hair around my finger.

I didn't realize how much I was hurting people. Is my mother right, am I dealing with my pain by being angry? I had so many questions running through my mind and I couldn't stop them. I heard the door open and I opened my eyes, hoping it was my mother coming back to explain to me what she was talking about, but it wasn't. It was the nurse coming in with the discharge papers.

My mother came back in the room as I was signing the papers. She walked over to the other side of the bed and finished packing my things. I finished signing the papers and gave them back to the nurse. She passed me my copy and flashed me a smile before leaving.

"You ready?" she asked as she grabbed my bags.

I took the bags outta her hands and motioned for her to sit down on the bed. She sat down with a puzzled look on her face.

"Can we talk?" I asked, taking her hand.

"Yeah, what's wrong?" she replied.

"What did you mean by the comment you made earlier?" She shook her head as she closed her eyes tightly.

"I can't do this right now, Venus," she said in a small voice.

"But, Ma, I feel like you're hiding something from me. I don't understand," I stated, perplexed.

"Just drop it, ok?" she snapped.

She jumped up, wrapping her arms around her waist.

"I can't talk about this right now, please, just leave it alone." Her voice was slightly above a whisper.

Whatever she was hiding must have brought back some horrible memories 'cause she was visibly shaken. I had a sinking feeling in the pit of my stomach, making me feel uncomfortable. Something about the way my mother was acting really bothered me, and I needed answers.

"Come on, Ma, tell me." She wiped tears from her eyes, then grabbed my bags.

"Is it really that bad?" She looked at me like she didn't know what I was talking about. "Your secret," I clarified.

"It's not a secret, just a painful memory that I tried to suppress," she replied.

"Tell me, Ma, please?" I pleaded with her. She leaned her head back as a tear rolled down the side of her face.

"I don't want to hurt you; you're going through enough right now and I don't want you to get angry," she said in a low voice.

"Ma, I can take it. Please, I need to know," I assured her.

"Baby, just let me take you home and we can talk about this another day. I promise, Venus, I'll tell you everything. I haven't had to face this without drugs yet and I need to make sure that I can handle it. I never wanted you to know, but I know it's time for me to tell you the truth. I just need a little more time."

I didn't want to push her anymore. I decided to drop the subject until she was ready to talk.

"Ok, Ma, I'll give you time. Just promise me that you will tell me the truth, I mean everything."

"I promise I will." I hugged her, she grabbed the rest of my bags and we left.

The car ride was silent. I stared out the window with a million and one questions running through my mind. I glanced at my mother; she was sitting stiff, gripping the steering wheel tight as hell with her eyes glued to the road. I turned towards the window and stared at trees, as usual, with thoughts of my missing child flooding my mind.

Adonis

Staring at the broken bottles of alcohol and pillows thrown all over the floor, an overwhelming feeling washed over me. I shook my head as I started cleaning up. Venus was coming home and I wanted everything to be perfect. I didn't want to give her a reason to lash out. I understand how she feels, and I even get why she blamed me for this situation. The lifestyle I live is ruthless, and most niggas in this life are heartless. But I don't know how much more of her attacks I can take.

"I wish you could understand, I feel the same anger you feel," I mumbled, as I picked up the picture of Venus off the shelf. I wiped my fingers over her face. "I blame myself too." I stared at her beautiful smile, wondering if I would ever see it again.

Thinking about the damage I did to my house the night before, I placed the picture back on the shelf and continued picking up the shards of glass. I buried my own anger deep inside, and allowed Venus to take hers out on me. But last night, I needed some kind of relief. I came in the house, poured myself a drink, and started thinking about my baby. Rage took over and I threw my glass, but that wasn't enough. I threw the pillows off the sofa; next thing I know, I knocked all the bottles off the glass mini bar, then broke that too.

As I swept up the last pieces of glass, the phone started ringing. I peeped over the coffee table, and my mother's name was displayed on the screen. I put the broom down and rushed to answer it.

"Hey, Ma, what's up?" I answered.

"Hi, Daddy," Harmony answered. Hearing my princess's voice brought a smile to my face.

"Hey, baby, what you doing?" I asked.

"Is mommy home yet?" She ignored my question. I snickered.

"No she's not home yet, but I promise she'll call you as soon as she gets settled," I replied.

"Ok, Daddy. I love you. Mwah," she giggled with her little snort, as she blew me a kiss. I laughed and blew her a kiss as well.

"I love you too, princess." I ended the call, then headed up the steps to clean the bedroom.

After cleaning the room and changing the sheets on the bed, I went down the hall to put the dirty sheets in the washer. Coming out of the laundry room, I walked past Serene's nursery. My heart dropped. I walked up to the door and took a deep breath before opening it.

Standing in the doorway of her nursery, blankly staring at the empty crib, wishing that she would magically appear, my heart and mind both began racing. Fear and anger struggled to take control of my heart, but my mind wouldn't let it. I know my baby is out there somewhere, waiting for her daddy to find her and bring her home.

"Daddy gon' find you, Serene, I promise," I whispered, as I walked over to her crib and picked up her blanket.

Cupping it tightly against my chest, I closed my eyes and held it up to my nose, and imagined breathing in her scent. I tried to paint a picture of her in my mind of what she would feel like cradled in my arms. I sat in the rocking chair and laid my head back. Typically, I'm not the type of nigga that just let my emotions out, but this shit right here got a nigga feeling broken deep inside.

"THIS SHIT AIN'T RIGHT!" I shouted as I threw the blanket back in the crib.

My chest started hurting as I stared at the colorful wooden letters on the wall, spelling out her name. I stood up and started walking around the room, looking at all the decorations. Venus really made this a room fit for a princess. I picked up the ceramic piggy bank and my rage came rushing to the surface.

Venus

I stood in the doorway, waving to my mother, as she pulled out of the driveway. I closed the door, then locked it behind me. I walked in the house and a heavy scent of Lysol cleaner mixed with a strong scent of alcohol invaded my nostrils. *What the hell?* I thought, as I stood in the middle of the foyer looking around the house. Something seemed to be outta place. I walked deeper into the house and started roaming around the living room. As my eyes darted around the room, I noticed that the glass mini bar was missing from the corner.

What the fuck happened? I wondered, noticing the trash bag full of glass. I opened it and saw the chrome trimming of the mini bar.

Suddenly, I heard a crash, then a loud thump coming from upstairs. It sounded like something hit the floor hard. My heart started racing as I rushed up the steps to see what was going on. I saw Adonis in the middle of the floor in the nursery, looking up in the sky. The ceramic piggy bank he bought her was laying on the floor in front of him, shattered in pieces. At first, I thought Adonis was praying, but as I stood at the door listening, I found that he was talking to Lavelle.

"Why in the hell did this shit happen to me? Why the fuck is my baby missing? Can you please tell me, what the hell did I do so fucking wrong?" His voice cracked as he spoke, and I could hear sorrow in his tone. "I hear your voice in my head telling me to hang in there, but I swear, Lavelle, this shit hurts like hell. I can't eat, can't sleep, shit, I can hardly breathe." He rubbed his hands over his face. "God, I wish you were here. I need you so much right now." He breathed. "Seeing Venus so hurt is killing me. I'm supposed to be strong for her, but how can I be strong when I'm so torn up inside." He let out a deep sigh before continuing. "I'm tired of pretending that I'm ok, like I have it all together. The truth is I don't, I can't even function. I drag myself out of bed every morning and put on this fake smile, when I'm secretly crying behind my eyes."

I wiped the tears from my eyes. Seeing him look so broken was tugging at my heart strings. I was so caught up in my own pain and anger that I couldn't see how this was affecting him. I walked over to him and touched his shoulder. He looked up at me, and I saw the pain in his eyes, the darkness from sleepless nights. He looked as if the weight of the world was sitting on his shoulders.

"I'm sorry," I apologized in a brittle voice.

I pulled him into my arms, holding his head against my stomach. He wrapped his arms around my waist as I burst into tears. He stood up and sat in the rocking chair. He grabbed my hands and pulled me down on his lap.

"We'll get through this as long as we're together." He pulled me closer to him and kissed me. He grabbed the back of my head pulling me deeper into the kiss.

"I missed you," he whispered into my mouth as our tongues massaged each other.

I felt my body starting to respond to his kiss. My body started quivering. I could feel his dick getting hard under me. I abruptly pulled away from his kiss and he chuckled.

"Now you know you got to wait six weeks for that," I raised my eyebrows.

"There's other things we can do," he smirked with a devilish grin. I shook my head, smiling.

"It's good to see you smiling," he said, as he stroked my cheek.

I got up and walked over to the crib. I picked up Serene's blanket and held it against my chest.

"I just want her back, Adonis," I stressed. He walked over to me and embraced me.

"I'll find her and bring her home. I promise," he pledged, cradling my head against his chest. "Harmony wants you to call her," he added, passing me his phone.

"Oh shit, Adonis. How are we gonna explain to Harmony why I don't have her little sister with me?" I asked with panic in my tone.

"Calm down, Venus, we'll find a way. Right now, just call her. She misses you." I sat down in the rocking chair and called Harmony.

"Hi, baby," I greeted her as soon as Mrs. Thompson put her on the phone.

"Hi, Mommy," she responded excitedly.

I laughed. Hearing her voice made me feel warm inside. I missed her. I talked to her for a few minutes, then I told her that I needed to lie down and get some rest. She made me promise that Adonis would come and get her later.

"She's probably gon' drive my mother crazy asking when she's coming home," Adonis chuckled.

I agreed. My phone vibrated in my hand; it was Kay Kay.

"Hey, Kay Kay, what's up?" I answered.

"I was checking on you, how you feeling?" she asked.

"Extremely tired. I'm about to try to get a little rest before Harmony comes home."

"Yeah, I was about to take a nap too," she yawned. "I'll call you a little later to check on you."

"Aight, talk to you later." Adonis came back in the room just as I was ending the call. He passed me two bottles of cold water. I opened the first one, and drunk it down as soon as I opened it. I was thirsty as hell. The other bottle I put on the nightstand next to me.

"I'm gon' let you lay down and get some rest," he said walking out the room, but I stopped him and told him that I wanted him to lie with me. Not only did I miss cuddling with him, but he looked exhausted and I needed him to be well rested to find my daughter.

Kay Kay

The loud banging on my door awakened me from my nap. I yawned and stretched. I looked at the clock and noticed I was only asleep for an hour.

Shit, I thought, as the banging started again. I got up from the couch.

"I'm coming!" I shouted, dragging myself to the door.

Patting my head rapidly trying to stop the itch, I yawned again. *Damn I'm tired as hell,* I thought. I opened the door. Loco was standing there with his arms folded across his chest.

"Hi," he greeted me, then brushed past me and entered the house.

I rolled my eyes and closed the door.

"What you doing here?" I asked, as I placed my hands on my hips.

"Man, Kay Kay, stop fuckin' playing with me. You know why the fuck I'm here," he snapped.

I shook my head and walked over to the couch and laid back down.

"Loco, it's been months since we saw each other. How in the hell am I supposed to know why you're here?" I yawned.

"Get yo' lazy ass up. What the fuck you still sleeping for at 2 o'clock?" he asked as he moved my feet off the couch.

"Loco, what do you want?" I was getting annoyed with him.

"You," he admitted. "I'm still yo' man, right?" he questioned.

"Are you?" I replied with a smug look. "I thought that by me not seeing and hardly talking to you for the past three months, you'd get the hint." I was really fuckin' with him. I'd only been pretending not to want to see him or talk to him. The truth is I was gonna call him and ask him to come see me tonight when I got up from my nap.

"I don't take hints. Tell me directly, are we done or not?" He had a serious look on his face and for some reason, that made me burst into laughter.

"Kaylee, what the fuck's so fuckin' funny?" he asked confused.

"You, Loco, you funny," I chuckled. I placed my hands on his distorted face. "Awww, my baby was lost without me," I giggled.

"Quit playing games and answer the damn question!" he barked, moving my hands from his face. I snickered one last time then got serious.

"No, Loco, we're not done. We were never done. I love yo' crazy ass to death, I just needed some time to figure out what to do about this situation without you hounding me," I replied.

"So it took you three months to figure that out?" he grilled.

"No, it didn't," I answered. "In fact, I made my decision after I went to the doctor and got all the information about my options. I just had an appointment like a little over a month ago," I explained.

"About that..." he started. He took a deep breath and ran his hand through his dreads then continued. "After seeing what Venus and Adonis is going through, I understand why you don't want to have my baby. I support your decision not to have it. I'll do whatever you need me to do."

"Good, I'm glad you said that. I was actually gonna call you today and ask if you would go with me. I'm nervous. I wasn't sure how you would respond." I shrugged my shoulders.

"Yeah, I'll go with you," he nodded his head as he answered.

I climbed on top of him, straddling him.

"I missed you, you know that?" I kissed him passionately. He wrapped his arms around my waist, pulling me closer as we got deeper into the kiss.

"I missed yo' simple ass too." He stroked my hair, then kissed me again.

He flipped me down on the couch and started kissing on my neck.

"Wait, nigga, I don't know what you been doing the last few months. You have a reputation of being a hoe," I stated matter-of-factly.

"All I been doing these last few months was waiting on you to stop this dumb shit. I ain't fuck nobody. This dick is for you." He looked me directly in the eyes when he said that. "You know you in trouble for playing with a nigga, right? My ass is backed up like a nigga 'bout to catch blue balls." He started pulling at the string to my sweatpants, trying to untie them quickly.

"So what, you gonna fuck me to sleep?" I asked jokingly.

"Fuck you to sleep?" he asked then snickered. "What I'm about to do to you, yo' ass gon' damn near die." He snatched my sweatpants and underwear down to my ankles. I stepped out of them, then he lifted my shit over my head.

"Even with that lil' potbelly, you sexy as fuck," he complimented, as he tugged at his belt to take it off. He pulled his shirt off.

I felt like I was drooling, staring at this handsome tatted up man with the body of a God. Then my eyes roamed down to that massive piece of grade A beef that was already standing at attention. My mouth started watering. I dropped to my knees and gave him a nice big kiss hello.

I licked around the shaft, getting it nice and wet like he likes it. Looking up into his eyes, I slowly sucked it into my mouth.

"MMMM!" he moaned as he tilted his head back. We had a lot of making up to do.

Loco

Staring down at those big beautiful eyes as Kay Kay made my dick disappear in her mouth, turned me on more than I already was. I grabbed the top of her head and guided her head up and down my pole.

"Yeah, baby, suck that dick like you love it," I said in a low tone.

She grabbed the shaft with both hands, twisting and stroking as she sucked on only the head. She was flicking her tongue in and out of the hole and making her long tongue twirl around the head. I closed my eyes, licked then bit my bottom lip. I could feel my heart pumpin' through my dick. She was topping me off exactly how I loved it: slow, wet, and deep as fuck. I grabbed her hands with both hands and started ramming my dick down her throat as far as I could. Fuck gag reflexes, I was tryna give her tonsils a workout.

"Yes, baby, just like that," I grunted, tryna hold back my nut.

"MMMMM!" she moaned. The vibrations from her moans made my dick harder.

She sped up the pace a little bit, gripping my waist and pulling me deeper.

"SSSSHIT!" I hissed as I shot cum down her throat. She looked up at me with sexy eyes as she licked the dripping nut from the hole.

I sat her down on the sofa and parted her legs. Sticking my fingers in her, I started playing with her, making sure she was nice and wet. I was ready to taste my baby. I missed the sweet taste of her pussy. I twirled my tongue around her pearl, sucking it gently.

"Damn, Loco," she whispered, opening her legs wider.

I started devouring her pussy. I licked her from hole to hole, asshole to elbows; I licks everything. As I stuck my tongue in her asshole, she started squirming and moaning loudly. All I wanted to do was slide up in her tight wetness.

I grabbed her legs and opened them as wide as they could go, then I slid my pole inside her. She was so tight, it felt like she was squeezing my dick.

"Got damn," I huffed as I forced my rod in a little further.

"OOOOWWW!" she screamed in pain.

I stroked in and out of her slowly until her body and pussy muscles started to flex. She started getting wetter and I was sliding in her with ease. I gripped her waist and plowed deeply inside of her.

"Oh shit, Loco, please stop," she begged.

"Fuck no, you getting all this shit. I got three months to make up for." I put her legs on my shoulders, gripped her waist, and pounded her hard and deep.

"Loco, fuck, oh my God, Loco!" She was hollering and screaming. Usually I'll tell her to stop that shit and handle my dick, but right now I don't give a fuck. Her pretty ass was balled up against this couch unable to move, so she had no other choice but to take this shit.

My knees were hurting on that hard ass wood floor, so I sat on the couch and pulled her on top of me. She straddled me and tried to ease down on the dick. I grabbed her around the waist and slammed into her. Her titties were bouncing, smacking me in my face as she bounced on my pole. I grabbed them both and start going back and forth, sucking on them. She grabbed the back of the couch for balance as she rocked her hips.

"Cum for me, cum on my dick. Yeah, baby, come on," I coached, as she threw her head back and let out a scream and released her juices all on my lap. But I wasn't done with her.

I turned her on all fours and went balls deep in her pussy.

"Fuck, Loco... Oh shit... Yessss, baby... gimme that dick." Her words echoed through the living room as she repeated them over and over again, gripping the blanket she had on the couch tightly.

Speeding up my strokes, I gripped her hips and plunged deeper in to her. She moaned loudly and she started bucking back, matching my stroke. I felt her body shaking violently.

"That's right, let it go," I coached, as I felt my own body tremble.

"MMM... MMM... MMM!" I grunted, as sweat dripped off my face to her ass.

"I missed this pussy," I whispered, spreading her ass cheeks so I could watch my dick slide in and out of her.

The trembles in my body got stronger, and her screams got louder. I thrusted hard one last time, and we both climaxed. I collapsed on the couch tryna catch my breath. She curled up next to me, and I could feel the heat from our bodies radiating between us.

"Damn, Loco, that was good as shit," she whispered, sounding exhausted. Shit, I was too. That was the biggest nut I had in a long ass time. She pulled the cover over us and we both fell asleep.

My body was aching like shit when I woke up a couple hours later. I slowly moved Kay Kay's head off my arm, carefully climbing over top of her. I noticed the little bulge in her stomach.

"Hey lil man or princess, this yo' daddy. I just want you to know that I'm sorry," I spoke into her belly. I kissed it lightly then headed to the kitchen.

I opened the freezer and smiled; my baby had a bottle of Henny in there waiting on me. I took the frosted bottle out of the freezer, opened it and took a gulp.

"Ain't nothing sexier than a naked man standing in the kitchen," Kay Kay giggled as she sat on the stool.

"Want some eggs?" I joked, mimicking Melvin from the movie *Baby Boy*. She started laughing.

"You stupid." She slid off the stool and started cooking dinner.

After eating steak, mashed potatoes with gravy, green beans, and blueberry muffins, a nigga had the itis like shit. I had to work that food outta me. I helped her clean the kitchen, then we headed upstairs to shower, and finished out an all-night fuck session.

The next day, we were sitting in the doctor's office waiting for Kay Kay's name to be called. I was honest when I said I supported her decision, but this shit was really fuckin' with me. These stupid ass people that run this damn office, thinks it's okay to have pregnant women and kids running around the office, while I'm in here so Kay Kay can kill my baby.

This some sick ass shit! I thought, as I glanced around at the walls full of pregnancy information. I looked over at Kay Kay and said "Why the hell they got all this pregnancy shit up when we here to get a fuckin' abortion?" I inquired.

"Loco, some women are here to have a baby, not an abortion. They have to accommodate them too," she whispered.

I understood what she was explaining, but this shit was fucked up and had a nigga in his feelings. I'm not built for this emotional shit. Kay Kay's lil' ass was changing me. I'ma have to stop that shit. She was making me feel soft.

"Kaylee Turner," the medical assistant called out.

Kay Kay jumped up, acting like she was all excited and shit. I was nervous as hell.

We walked down the hallway and went into the second room on the left. The assistant told Kay Kay to change into her gown. She started undressing as I slid my arms around her waist.

"Yo' sexy ass lucky we waiting on the doctor 'cause I'd bend yo' ass over right now," I whispered in her ear.

"Boy, get off me," she giggled, bumping me away.

I sat in the chair and watched her finish undressing. She started wiggling her hips like a stripper. When she was all the way undressed, she started twerking. I shook my head.

"I'm glad you can find humor when you getting ready to have this procedure done," I pointed out.

"Orlando Tyrell Gains, just sit there and be quiet." She loves saying my whole damn government.

She slid on the table, swinging her legs, waiting for the doctor. I started looking around at all the posters and pamphlets. I really don't get it; why have all this type of shit when you're doing abortions? The doctor came in the room. She was a petite Indian woman with jet black hair that came almost to her ass.

"Hi, how are you doing, mom?" she asked, smiling.

"I'm doing good," Kay Kay replied. "Doctor Bhatti, this is Orlando, the father," she introduced.

I got up and shook the doctor's hand and greeted her.

"So you ready?" she asked Kay Kay. She nodded yes, then the doctor left the room.

"Oh, Loco, I gotta tell you something before I do this," Kay Kay said as she reached for my hand.

"What's up?" I asked taking her hand.

"I decided to keep the baby, we not here for an abortion. We're here for a sonogram," she admitted.

She was grinning from ear to ear. I was stunned.

"Wait, you planned this?" I asked. She nodded with a goofy ass grin on her face.

"Sorry I lied," she apologized, shrugging her shoulder. "I wanted to surprise you. I'm 17 weeks pregnant, and today we might find out the sex of the baby. Don't be mad at me," she whined, pouting.

I was not mad at all, I was excited. I never thought about having a child until I got out of this lifestyle, but Kay Kay made me want those things and more. She got a nigga thinking of marriage and all. Moving to a nice suburban area in a nice house with a big backyard for the kids and having cookouts. That unrealistic ass TV life shit. I want that with her.

Before I could respond to her, the doctor and her assistant came in rolling a machine with a monitor on it. Kay Kay slid on the table, and the doctor put some gel stuff on her then rolled this handle across her stomach.

"There's the baby," Doctor Bhatti pointed to the screen.

I was in awe looking at the image of my child. It was the most amazing thing I had ever seen. I was smiling so hard my cheeks started to hurt, then she turned up the volume on the machine. Whooshing sounds came blurring through the speakers, then I heard sounds, almost like horse galloping.

"What's that sound?" I asked.

"That's your baby's heartbeat," Doctor Bhatti replied. "And it's very strong," she added.

"Yeah, he's strong like his daddy," I beamed proudly. Kay Kay rolled her eyes.

"You don't know it's a boy," she said, shaking her head. "Doctor Bhatti, can you tell the sex?" Kay Kay asked.

The doctor rolled the handle over Kay Kay's stomach, then she pointed to the screen.

"You see that right there? That's his penis. Daddy was right, you're having a boy," she announced.

"Oh, hell yeah!" I cheered.

Kay Kay laughed and said, "Oh please," rolling and cutting her eyes at me.

I couldn't stop smiling. I kept peeking at the screen at my boy. I swear a tear fell from my eye.

The doctor printed out the images and gave them to me. I couldn't stop staring at them.

After the doctor left the room, I grabbed Kay Kay and embraced her. My love for her grew that day.

"I think we need one of these tables in our house. Imagine the things I could do with your feet in the stir ups." I kissed her on the back of her neck.

"Our house? So we gon' get a house together?" she asked, turning to face me.

"Yeah, we doing this shit right." I was dead ass. I was ready to give her everything she wanted.

"So you not upset with me for tricking you?" she asked, as I held her in my arms.

"Oh, you gon' pay for that, but I'm the happiest man in the world right now. Lil' Loco gon' be just like his daddy. You see the size of his dick?" I beamed.

"You got problems," she chuckled as I kissed her.

"I love you," she stated.

"Yeah, that part," I replied.

"You so simple," she laughed, playfully slapping my arm. I pulled her into my arms.

"I can't wait to tell everybody 'bout my lil' man. I'm already a proud papa and he ain't even here yet." She shook her head, grabbed my hand and we walked out.

A week later

Beans

I hate doing fuckin' stakeouts, I thought, sitting in the closet in the guest bedroom of Tekelia's house.

I was waiting for her to get home from work. I'd been following her for a week, learning her schedule and her daily routine, studying every part of her life. I needed to find out when would be the best day and time to snatch her. Normally, she came straight home from work, but tonight she's almost two hours late.

"Come on, bitch, where the fuck are you?" I whispered, looking down at my watch.

It was starting to get hot in that closet. I didn't want to drip any sweat on her shit and leave my DNA behind.

I heard the front door open and close.

"SHIT!" she shouted. It sounded like she dropped something on the floor, then I heard her scrambling around in the kitchen.

This has got to be the slowest bitch in the world, I thought to myself. It was taking her forever to bring her ass up the steps.

I slowly opened the closet door and eased out, walking softly so I wouldn't be heard. I crept behind the door and waited for her to come upstairs. A few minutes later, I heard her humming and walking up the steps. She walked past the door. I crept behind her.

WHACK! I hit her with the butt of my gun, knocking her out cold.

***

"MMMMM!" she moaned, blinking her eyes rapidly trying to focus.

"Where am I?" Her voice was faint. She blinked a few more times and noticed me sitting in the chair watching her. She gasped, damn near jumping outta her skin.

"Who the fuck are you? What do you want?" she questioned, struggling to free herself from the ropes that had her bound to the chair.

"Why am I here?" she asked.

Her voice was brittle as her chest started to rise and fall rapidly.

"Please don't hurt me," she begged.

"You'll be fine as long as you answer my questions," I lied. I had no intentions on letting this bitch live.

"I don't know what you can possibly need from me," she spoke as if she was baffled.

"ANSWERS!" I shouted, pulling out the picture I printed from the footage. "Who the fuck is this?" I inquired.

"Sh... She's the baby's mother," she lied.

SMACK! I hit her across the face with the back of my hand.

"Don't fuckin' try to play me," I spoke calmly. I held the picture up again. "Tell me what you know about her."

"Really, I don't know who she is," she fibbed.

I'm really not in the business of beating on women, but this bitch is about to make me fuck her up.

"If you don't start talking now, I promise you won't live to see another day," I threatened.

Her breathing became labored, and her eyes filled with tears. She still wouldn't talk, so I had decided to try another way to get her talking. I pulled out my bone cutters, and placed her pinky inside.

"Oh God, please don't do this?" she pleaded, tears streaming down her face.

"AAAAAAHHHHH!" she howled as her finger dropped to the floor. "YOU SICK BASTARD!" she cried out. I cut off another finger.

Her body trembled from the tremendous amount of pain she was in. I grabbed a hand full of her hair, snatching her head back.

"Look, bitch, I'm not fuckin' around. Tell me what the fuck I want to know or I will do things to your body and make you suffer in ways you never thought was possible." I spoke in a barbarous tone, giving her a cynical look.

He heart was beating so fast I could see it pulsating in her neck.

"We could do this all night." A sadistic smile grew over my face as I pulled out a hunting knife.

"Have you ever heard of lingchi?" She shook her head. I slowly walked around her chair. "It means death by a thousand cuts." I stopped in front of her and placed the knife against her cheek. "It's a slow and painful death." I leaned so close to her I could feel her breath mixed with mine. "Like I said, I got all night." I sliced her cheek about a half of an inch.

"AAAAAhhhhhh!" She was in agony.

She started crying, sweating profusely, while her body trembled. She slowly blinked her eyes.

"Ok, I'll talk," she cried, holding her head down. "The woman in the picture name is Ashley Brooks," she sniffed.

"How do you know her?" I asked.

"We went to nursing school together," she answered.

"Tell me how did you get involved with this kidnapping?" I interrogated.

"I needed the money badly. My mother was sick and I needed the money to pay for her care. Ashley knew it and offered me $30,000 to help her." She paused. "I was supposed to cut the ID band off of the mother's wrist and give it to Ashley. When she came to get the baby, I was to follow the normal procedures and give her the baby." Tears dripped from her face to her shirt.

"I'm sorry," she whispered.

"Where's Ashley now?" I asked.

"I don't know." I sliced her face again. She screamed.

"TELL ME THE FUCKIN' TRUTH!" I yelled.

"I am telling you the truth. She gave me a key to a P.O. box, that's how she paid me. She said we can't contact each other for a while." She was staring me dead in my eyes. I can tell she was telling the truth. I stood in silence why I processed the information.

"I told you everything I know. Please, just let me go," she pleaded with a tremulous voice. She was in so much pain.

It was time for me to take her out of her misery. I walked behind her, grabbed her head, holding it backwards as I slit her throat. As she bled out, I turned on the incinerator. I walked back over to her body, slumped in the chair. I picked her and the chair up and threw them both in the incinerator. Then I hosed the ground, removing all her blood. After cleaning up and making sure there was no evidence of her being there, I shut off the incinerator and headed back to my spot to run traces on Ashley Brooks.

Havoc

"Yo, Havoc, what's going on with that nigga in D.C.? It's been months since they ran up in our shit talkin' 'bout we work for him now, but we ain't get no supply yet. We can't serve our customers, they goin' somewhere else. This some bullshit, Havoc, and you know it." Floyd was pissed and so was the rest of my team.

I reached out to Alexia, but them niggas had her shook. They killed Maurice and sent her his skinned off tattoo, so she says she's out. Shit's been real fucked up 'round here. I don't know what them niggas did, but no muthafuckin' body wants to supply us. The ones that will, their products are some bullshit. My team is dry as fuck and I need to handle this shit like right the fuck now.

"Floyd, I got this. Get this together while I make this phone call. We need to have a meeting."

Floyd left the room, and I called my friend in D.C. I sat back in the chair waiting for the ringing phone to be answered.

"Yo, what's the word? My niggas hungry and we can't get work. That bitch, Alexia, bailed on us, and niggas looking at us like we on some bullshit. What the fuck you gon' do about that? You keep saying be patient, well my patience is gone. I want to handle them muthafuckas and build my shit back up myself," I ranted as soon as the phone was answered.

"Look, I said I got you. I need to tie up a few things then I'll be back home to get us that work. But you right, them niggas need to be handled. I'm sending someone to help with the plan; they know a lot about the niggas. Them niggas ruthless, they will never let y'all take over their shit unless they're dead. They're vulnerable right now so the time to take them out is now."

"Aight, I'll sit tight for a few days." I ended the call. I was glad to know Ash still had my back.

Returning to the front of the house where my crew was all gathered together, talking shit to each other, I cleared my throat, making my presence be known. The chatter between the group of men ceased. All eyes were on me as I made my way to the head of the table.

"Niggas out here serving our customers on our fuckin' turf. How the fuck does that make us look? Are we some bitch ass niggas? Hell no! Are we gon' lay down and let niggas fuck us? Hell fuckin' no. We gon' get them niggas in D.C., then we gon' come home and reclaim our shit. Ash sending somebody here to give us info on them bitch ass D.C. niggas. Get yo' shit together and yo' minds right. We hungry, niggas, act like it." I got straight to the point. I got up from the table and headed back to my office. I needed to make some moves before going to handle business.

"Yo, Havoc, you know I ride with you, but I need to know that this shit gonna pay off for me. I got a girl and two kids that I need to provide for, and this bullshit job I got ain't cutting." Craig was whining when he spoke. I started to slap his bitch ass.

"Look, nigga, stop sounding like a bitch. I got you. You ride with me, we finna get paid. We takin' our turf back and gon' take over other niggas' shit. I told y'all asses I'ma show muthafuckas I ain't to be fucked with," I told him.

"Aight, Havoc. I just got a fucked up feeling but I'm in," he assured me. He left my room.

This bitch, Ashley, better come through, 'cause niggas is countin' on me, and I can't let these niggas down. I have to smoke that nigga, Adonis, and his whole fuckin' team.

Venus

"I still can't believe you're gone, my angel. Even though I held you only once, I still remember how you felt in my arms. I hope you're ok. I hope whoever has you loves you as much as I do. I miss you so much. Daddy is doing all he can to find you and bring you home where you belong. Your dad will never stop looking for you and he will stop at nothing to get you back. So hang in there my precious baby; we'll be together soon, I hope. Remember, Mommy loves you." I folded her blanket and put it back in the crib. I stood in the doorway, looking around the room one more time before closing the door.

Getting back to a normal routine had been challenging. It had been three weeks and we were no closer to finding Serene as we were the day she went missing. I find myself thinking about her a lot, then I feel depressed. I can hardly get out of bed some days, and the off and on crying spells are tearing me to pieces. If it wasn't for Harmony, I wouldn't have the strength to push through each day.

"Mommy, Mommy, Mommy!" Harmony called, running down the hallway.

"Yes, sweetheart," I answered, as I sat down on my bed. I was feeling kind of down today.

"Can you take me to the park?" she asked excitedly.

"Not today. Mommy's not feeling well," I explained.

"You never feel well," she pouted, folding her arms across her chest.

"Hey you, what's with the attitude?" I questioned. She started walking out of my room. "Get back here, Harmony," I commanded.

She came back over and sat on my bed.

"What's wrong? Talk to me," I insisted.

"You don't play with me anymore." She poked out her bottom lip. I almost burst into laughter, but I contained myself.

"Awww, my little chocolate drop. Mommy is so sorry, but my body has to finish healing. I'm a lot better, but not completely well. I promise that mommy will be better soon and I will be running around here playing with you again." I kissed her on the top of her head. "You know what mommy can do?"

"What?" she asked with a grin.

"I can... do this." I started planting kisses all over her face and tickling her.

She was squirming and giggling all over the bed. Her little giggle was the best sound I've heard in a long time.

The doorbell rang, interrupting our playtime. I pulled her up off the bed.

"Let's go see who's at the door," I said, and she took off running.

"Slow down, little girl," I called behind her as I made my way down the hall.

"Who is it?" she asked at the door.

She turned the knob on the door, trying to open it.

"Hey, you know you don't open the door. Let it go now," I scolded.

"It's Grandma," she stressed jumping up and down.

I didn't know which grandma she was referring to, my mother or Adonis's. Either way, she was excited. She loved them both. I opened the door.

"Ma, what you doing here?" I was surprised because she never popped up at my house.

"I came to see you and my lil' tink tink here," she said picking up Harmony.

"Spoiled self." I playfully popped her on the leg.

We went into the living room and sat on the sofa. Harmony's mouth was running a mile a minute, telling my mother all about *The Princess and the Frog* movie. I sat in silence, shaking my head. It ain't like we haven't seen that and the *Frozen* movie a million times already. One of them stays in Harmony's DVD player.

"Sweetie, can you do grandma a huge favor?" Harmony nodded. "Can you go to your room so grandma and mommy can talk? I promise when I leave, you can go with me so you can see Auntie Layna."

"YAAAY!" Harmony cheered before running up to her room.

"That child is a ball of energy," I chuckled.

I turned towards my mother, and she had a look of sadness on her face. I was concerned.

"What's going on, Ma?" I inquired.

She let out a loud sigh, wiping her hands on her jeans. I sat back waiting for her to get herself together enough to tell me what was on her mind.

"I never wanted to tell you this," she started. She paused and took another deep breath, taking my hands in hers. "At the hospital you questioned me about saying I hope you never know my pain. I knew then that I was gonna have to tell you sooner or later. Keeping the truth from you was no longer an option."

I was scared to hear what she had to say. She got so upset at the hospital, and now she's looking like she's about to cry. I've never seen her look so broken before. She ran her hand through her hair before continuing.

"I wanted to go to college, it was my dream. When I was a senior in high school, I had an opportunity to attend a program that allows weekend visits to college to try to see which one is right for you. After the tour of the campus, we were assigned to dorms. That night I met a couple, a guy and a girl. We hung out and clicked, I felt comfortable with them. They invited me to a party the next day." She paused, closing her eyes tightly. A lone tear rolled down the corner of her eye. "I was 18 and it was the first time I was away from home. I wanted to have fun." She dropped her head and sat motionless.

I patiently waited for her to continue the story, unsure if I really wanted to know. Tears dripped off her chin, but she wiped them away.

"I was drinking a lot; it was my first time drinking. It hit me hard. I started feeling dizzy and the girl told me that I could go upstairs and lie down. I couldn't walk straight. The guy and the girl helped me to the room and closed the door. The girl lifted my skirt, I pulled it down." She started shedding tears again.

She looked at me with tears flooding her face, and she continued. "I said no, I kept saying no, but I was too drunk. They held me down and the girl did oral sex on me." She shook her head. "He watched, and when she was finished, he raped me too." By this time, I couldn't hold back my own tears. She looked so hurt. "After he finished, he opened the door and yelled something in the hallway. Next thing I know, I was being raped over and over by different men." She covered her mouth with her hand, weeping heavily. "I don't know how many men, and they kept coming in and out. I kept blacking out and waking back up to a different man." I held her while she wept in my arms. My heart was breaking for her.

"Ma, I'm so sorry that happened to you," I said, apologizing in a low brittle voice.

"There's more. The next morning, I woke up in the lobby of the dorm. My body was sore, and flashes of that night were clouding my head. I tried to deal with it on my own. I hid it from everybody, until I couldn't hide it anymore." Her voice was distant and so was the look in her eyes.

I told her that we didn't have to talk about it anymore, but she insisted to go on. What she told me next was a heartbreak that nothing could prepare me for.

"I got pregnant from that rape, but no one would believe me," she stated in a flat voice as she squeezed my hand tightly.

To say I was stunned was an understatement. I burst into tears, realizing what my mother was telling me. "No, Ma, don't tell me that, please," I sobbed. My chest was so heavy, it felt like it was about to cave in.

"Venus, understand that I loved you in spite of where you came from. I don't know which one of those men are your father, but it didn't matter to me. You were mine," she cried.

My chest was hurting so bad that it made it difficult for me to breathe. I laid down on the sofa with my knees pulled to my chest. I was so hurt. My father was a rapist, a filthy, perverted ass nigga. I started crying my eyes out while my mother stroked my back.

"Taking drugs was the only thing that got rid of the pain. I never wanted to tell you any of this, Venus. I didn't want you to be hurt like you are now." She laid her head on my thigh. I placed my arm around her and we wept together.

Adonis

The faint sounds of sniffling echoed off the walls when I walked in the house. I called out to Venus, but she didn't answer. As I got closer to the living room, the sniffles turned into cries. Venus was lying on the sofa in the fetal position, crying. I rushed over to her and scooped her up in my arms.

"What's wrong?" I asked, brushing her hair from her face.

Her eyes were swollen and bloodshot, her nose was red, and a stream of tears was pouring out of her eyes.

"Talk to me, please," I pleaded. I was thinking her sadness was because of Serene.

She's been having days where she cries a lot, or she's depressed.

"It's just too much, Adonis. I can't take any more of this shit. I'm tired of having my heart broken over and over again. I feel like I'm gonna snap. I'm exhausted mentally, physically, and definitely emotionally," she sobbed into my chest. Her voice was muffled as she continued. "I just want some happiness. Every time I get a little bit of it, something always takes it away and fucks shit up for me. First, all the shit I've been through with you, having my baby kidnapped, and now this shit. When is it gonna end?" she broke down. I embraced her tighter and I rubbed her back for comfort.

"What happened today?" I asked, pulling her away from me.

The sadness in her eyes let me know the she was broken, and I had to be the one to fix her.

"Talk to me, please. I can't help you unless you tell me what's wrong," I spoke in a sincere tone.

"Sorry, Adonis, but you can't do shit about this," she said in a flat voice.

She let out a sigh. "Fuck my life!" she shouted.

"Baby, talk," I demanded.

She laid her head on the back of the sofa as tears filled her eyes. She began telling me her mother's story. It was sickening. Ms. Bowman is like my own mother. I know she was fucked up on drugs and did fucked up shit, but I loved her regardless. Hearing that something so horrible happened to her had my blood boiling. I wish I knew who those niggas were; I'd kill all of them.

Not only does Venus have to deal with the fact that she is the product of a rapist, but she has to come to terms with the fact that she would never know who he is. I feel fucked up inside. I know Levar is a piece of shit, but at least I know the nigga's name and who the fuck he is. She grew up not knowing who her father is and dealt with that, but hearing it could be one of the many perverted ass niggas who raped her mother is heart wrenching.

My phone vibrated and Beans's name showed on the display. He must have some information on the bitch who kidnapped my baby, but as much as I wanted to hear what he had to say, Venus needed me. I rejected the call. Noticing the house was extremely quiet, I asked where was Harmony.

"She went with my mother," she replied.

"You want to go lie down?" I asked. She nodded yes.

I walked her upstairs, and put her in the bed. Beans was calling my phone again. For him to call back to back, it must have been important. I answered it.

"Beans, what's going on?" I answered.

"I need you to meet me at my spot as soon as possible." He spoke with a hint of urgency.

"I'm dealing with something right now; I'll call you when I'm done," I replied.

"Sooner rather than later," he responded, letting me know time was of the essence.

I ended the call then turned my attention back on Venus. I pulled the blanket up on her and asked if she needed anything.

"No, but that phone call seemed important. Was it about Serene?" she inquired.

"I don't know, but I can meet with him later; right now, you need me." I leaned down and gave her a soft kiss.

"I'm fine, Adonis. I need you to find our daughter. That's the most important thing right now, and if that call was about her, you need to go," she stated. "Kay Kay's coming over in a few anyway. Go, I'll be alright."

I leaned down and gave her another kiss, then told her to call me if she needs me. She agreed. I started to leave the room. I turned around and walked back over to her and sat beside her.

"Let's get married soon," I said.

She gave me a puzzled look.

"What you mean?" she asked.

"You heard me, let's get married soon," I reiterated.

"How can I plan a wedding with everything going on?" she questioned.

"That's the thing, planning our wedding can take our minds off of the situation. Give us both some relief," I explained.

"I don't know, Adonis. Can I have some time to think about it?" I kissed her on the forehead.

"That's all I'm asking." I kissed her passionately before leaving.

***

"What you got for me, Beans?" I inquired as soon as I walked in.

"I paid the nurse a visit. She gave me the name of the bitch that has your daughter," he told me.

"You sure?" I asked.

"Her name is Ashley Brooks; does that name mean anything to you?" I repeated the name over and over in my head, tryna see if it did.

"Nah, that bitch don't sound familiar," I replied.

"Well, I'm gonna run her name in my system and tail her until I have all the information for you," he informed.

I sat down in the chair beside him and waited on the information.

"Beans, give me that nurse's info so I can handle that problem."

"It's already handled," he stated in a toneless voice.

"What you mean?" I asked with a perplexed look.

Beans worked with me and Lavelle for years, and outta all these years, I've never known Beans to be the type that got his hands dirty. I was shocked.

"Beans, what type of shit you on? I ain't never seen you get involved like that. I want details, nigga. What the fuck you do to that bitch?"

"Let's just say that the hospital gonna need a new nurse. The bitch disappeared without a trace." I started laughing, but this nigga was dead ass.

The computer flashed a match. Ashley Brooks' name, address, phone number, and everything else I needed was on the screen.

"I'll handle this bitch, Beans," I stated, writing down her information.

"Let me tail her for a few days, then get back to you with her schedule and daily routine," he suggested.

"Aight, do that, and I'll take care of everything else," I stressed.

"Ok, but if you need me, don't hesitate." He gave me a serious ass look.

"I got you, Beans." I gave him dap, then passed him the envelope containing his pay.

"Good luck on finding Serene." I thanked him, then left out.

That nigga Beans be on his shit, I thought, driving down the highway heading home. With the information Beans gave me, I was feeling hopeful. We were one step closer to finding Serene, and I couldn't wait to tell Venus. She needed something to cheer her up.

"Ashley Brooks, who the fuck is you?" I asked myself, wondering if I knew anybody in the streets with the name Brooks. I searched my brain over and over and still couldn't think of nobody.

Is this a random kidnapping, or was I a target? Why would you come after my daughter? Those questions kept running through my mind. The way it was planned out, it had to have something to do with me. I didn't have any enemies, so I don't understand this shit at all. The only person that I deal with that is capable to pull some shit like this off is Rojas, but we do good business together. He even called and thanked me for delivering Maurice's head to him. He said it showed him that I was a man of my word and he liked that about me.

"Hell no, Rojas didn't do this; his ass would've just had my ass killed. Plus, he had no reason to do some fucked up shit like this, we make a killing together." I realized that I was thinking out loud. This shit got me going crazy.

I turned up the volume on the radio, hoping to drown out my thoughts. I felt like Venus, I needed some relief.

I pulled in the driveway just as Kay Kay was opening her car door.

"What's up, Adonis?" she spoke as I was getting out of my truck.

"What's up? How you doing?" I questioned as I approached her.

"I'm good, you talk to yo' boy today?" she asked.

"Nah, I been in and out all day. Why, what's up?"

"I'll let him tell you." She closed her car door and started the engine, waving as she pulled out of the driveway.

I walked in the house, poured myself a drink, then made my way to the bedroom. Venus was lying across the bed, looking sexy as fuck in her short pajama shorts and tank top. A nigga was getting bricked up like shit.

"What's Kay Kay so fuckin' happy for?" I inquired, sitting on the bed beside her.

"She decided to keep the baby," she answered dryly.

"That's what's up. So that nigga gon' be somebody's daddy. What the hell this world coming to?" I laughed.

Venus didn't respond.

"Baby, what's wrong?" I kissed her on the top of her head, then rubbed her back.

"Kay Kay just laid a lot of stuff on my mind, and now I'm thinking about Serene." Her voice sounded as if she been crying.

"Speaking of Serene, I got some information." Venus hopped up quick as shit.

"Tell me," she said excitedly.

"The nurse, Tekelia, was in on the kidnapping," I started.

"What?" she cut me off.

"Yeah, she cut yo' wristband off and gave it to the bitch, but I have her information, baby. I'm gon' pay that bitch a visit and she better either have our baby, or tell me where the fuck she is," I barked.

"If she wants to live she will," Venus added.

"That bitch gon' die either way." I pulled Venus on my lap.

"We one step closer, baby." She grabbed my face and kissed me.

I tried to touch her tonsils with my tongue. She pulled away.

"No, Adonis, you know we can't do that for three more weeks." She tried to get up off my lap, but I pulled her back down.

"Just let me taste it," I said in a low seductive voice.

"No, we ain't doing nothing for three more weeks." I took her hand and placed it on my already hard dick.

"You feel that? He ain't waitin' no three fuckin' weeks." She started cracking up, but I was dead ass.

"Ain't nobody fooling with you, Adonis." She tried to get up again, but I grabbed her by the waist and sat her on my hardness, poking her in the ass.

"What you gon' do 'bout that?" I asked.

"Not a damn thing," she replied.

I flipped her over on the bed and pinned her hands over her head. I stuck my hand in her shorts. Feeling her wetness, I slid my fingers in to her sweet spot. She licked her lips as she let out a light guttural moan.

"See, you want it too," I mumbled, kissing her neck.

"I didn't say I don't want it, I said I can't for three weeks," she stressed.

"Man, fuck that six weeks' shit; we can do it. I'll take it slow," I insisted.

"No!" she answered.

She tried to wiggle from under me, but I wasn't giving up that easy. She forgot that I knew her body and I knew how to make her give in to my demands. Still pinning her arms over her head with one hand, I pulled her shirt up and started flicking her hard nipples with my tongue. She started squirming. I continued to finger her as I sucked her breasts.

"MMMMM!" she moaned as I felt her body relax.

She opened her legs a little wider so I could stick my finger deeper inside. She started thrusting her hips.

"Tell me you want me," I breathed into her mouth as I traced her lips with my tongue.

"Adonis." She whispered my name in a sexy ass tone. I felt that shit penetrate my body.

As my tongue twirled around in her mouth, she moaned, turning me on more than I already was. I looked up at her and she had a lustful thirst in her eyes.

"I want you," she moaned, rolling her eyes in her head.

I pulled her shorts and panties down in one quick yank. I parted her legs with my knees and dived my head in to her sweetness.

"MMMM, that feels so fuckin' good," she whimpered.

I pushed her knees back as my tongue twirled around her clit. She started fuckin' my mouth as her body trembled lightly.

"I'm about to cum already." Her voice trembled as she spoke.

"Oh shit, Adonis," she groaned.

I started feasting on her pussy, licking, sucking, and lightly nibbling on her pearl. She was squirming, jerking, and breathing so hard, it sounded like she was panting.

"FUUUUCK!" she shouted, as she grabbed my head and released in my mouth.

I was ready to dig in her guts. I pulled my jeans off, pushed her knees back and slowly slid my pole in to her wet, tight box. She grimaced in pain.

"Damn, baby, you tight as a muthafucka," I grunted, pushing my pole deeper inside.

For somebody who just had a baby, she was as tight as a virgin.

"Fuck, Venus," I huffed. I was already feeling like I was about to bust.

I bit down on my bottom lip as she grabbed my waist, pulling me deeper. She opened her legs wider. I thought she wanted me to go slow but she was just as hungry as I was.

I raised up off her a little and started pounding her with short, quick thrusts.

"AHH, AHHH!" she howled, clawing at my back.

"Shit, you feel so fuckin' good," I said as I started moving in a circular motion.

The sounds of our bodies smacking together mixed with our heavy breathing filled the room.

"Fuck me harder, Adonis," she commanded. That let me know that she needed this as much as I did.

I raised up on my knees, as she opened her legs in a wide V. I grabbed her and started plowing in her deep and hard.

"Oh, yessssss!" she cried out as tears trickled out of the corner of her eye.

I sped up my pace, and she started fuckin' me back hard. As we continued at that pace, our breathing became harder. She put her hands on my chest, gripping it tightly. That shit hurt like hell but I ignored it. I placed my hands on the side of her in the push-up position, and long stroked her while we stared into each other's eyes. No words needed to be spoken; our eyes were saying a lot. It felt like we connected on a different level of intimacy. We held each other's gaze as our bodies started trembling wildly.

"FUUUCK!" we shouted in unison, as we released together.

I collapsed on top of her, trying to catch my breath. She wrapped her legs and arms around me, and started kissing the top of my head.

"Yes, Adonis, I'll marry you soon," she whispered in my ear as she held me tighter.

Crazy ass flashed on the display of my ringing phone. It was Loco.

"My nigga, what the hell you doing?" I answered cheerfully. I was happy to hear he was gonna be a daddy.

"Shit," he replied. "You know Kay Kay keeping my baby, and it's a boy," he boasted.

"That's what's up! Congratulations, nigga. Meet me at Virgo Lounge tomorrow evening, we can celebrate a little." He agreed and we ended the call. Venus was asleep. I pulled the blanket over her, climbed in bed and went to sleep behind her.

Anonymous...

"Ummm, daddy! Yes, fuck me with that big dick," I moaned, pretending to enjoy the whack ass sex I was getting from one of my regulars.

"Yeah, you like this thing all in you, don't you?" he grunted like he was actually putting in work.

Thing? Are we fuckin' kids? I thought, looking back at him like he was stupid. I don't know why a lil' dick nigga needed a bitch to stroke his ego. You know yo' ass working with a baby dick.

"Yes, daddy, fuck me hard. You hurting my pussy, daddy," I whined, knowing good and got damn well I didn't feel shit.

SMACK! He smacked me on the ass.

"I want you to cum for daddy, I own this pussy." I rolled my eyes, I was bored as hell. He spread my ass cheeks. "I love how my cock looks going in you."

Cock? Did this corny ass muthafucka just say cock? I thought, twisting my face in disgust.

I wanted this nigga to hurry the fuck up. I had another john coming a little later, and I loved fuckin' him. He actually had a huge dick and made me have multiple orgasms. This non fuckin' muthafucka was pounding away inside me like a jack hammer, and I still didn't feel shit.

"OOOOHHH YEAH, DADDY, I'M ABOUT TO CUM!" I screamed and started faking like I was trembling, making all these fake ass moaning noises.

"Yeah, cum on this big black cock," he grunted.

This nigga said cock again. What type of fake ass porn this lil' dick having, no pussy getting ass nigga watch? Then this muthafucka got the nerve to have stamina. What a fuckin' waste!

I was tired of sex with his boring ass, so I started throwing my ass back.

"Oh yeah, aw yeah, fuck me back, baby, make that ass clap on my cock." I actually chuckled at that. If this nigga say cock one more time, I'm shootin' his black ass.

"AAAAAAAHHH!" I screamed and started jerking my body wildly. I faked an orgasm. "Let me suck that nut out for you, daddy," I purred.

I turned around and sucked him into my mouth.

"Aw shit, girl, whooo!" he howled.

To speed up his nut, I started jerking him off while sucking on his pole.

"Oh yeah, fuck, shit, got damn." He didn't know what the fuck to say as he shot his cum down my throat.

"Damn girl, you worth every bit of this $300." He breathed heavily. I always charged him more 'cause he couldn't fuck, had a lil' dick, and he was a waste of my time.

The baby started crying. Usually if I was fuckin' one of my dick slangin' regulars, I would've been pissed. But with this nigga, her crying was a blessing. I rushed his ass out of my house, ran in the bathroom and brushed my teeth.

"Mommy's coming, sweetheart," I mumbled as I rinsed the dripping toothpaste out of my mouth.

"Awww, mommy's here," I spoke softly, picking my baby up. I cradled her in my arms.

"You want a bottle?" I cooed, bouncing her lightly as I headed to the kitchen.

"You know I hate feeding you bottles. Breastmilk is best, but mommy don't have none of that, do she?" I kissed her on the tip of her nose.

"I can't wait 'til I can stop hiding you, but that can't happen until yo' parents die."

She started shifting and whining in my arms.

"SSSHHH! Stop fussing, baby, yo' bottle coming soon." I bounced her a little harder to calm her.

"You know mommy gonna take good care of you, right?" I watched as she balled her tiny little fists and held them against her face, slurping down her bottle.

"You are extremely adorable, looking like your daddy. My lil' honey colored bundle of sweetness." She stared at me with her big beautiful amber colored eyes.

"You're such a sweet baby," I glowed, stroking her chubby little cheek.

The phone vibrated on the coffee table, interrupting my bonding time with my daughter.

"What?" I answered.

"We have a problem to handle."

"What's the problem?"

After telling me what happened and giving me instructions, I came up with the perfect solution to all of our problems. I ended the call then picked up my baby.

"We have to change our plans, little one. Mommy don't have to trick anymore. I got something better for us. First thing in the morning, we're going to the airport."

Loco

"Shit, Kaylee. I don't know if it's the pregnancy hormones or what, but this shit feels good as muthafucka," I breathed, rolling off of her.

She climbed on top of me, straddling me.

"I don't know if it's the pregnancy hormones or what, but I want to fuck again." She leaned down and kissed me gently.

I ran my hands up and down her back, grabbed the back of her head, and pulled her deeper into the kiss. She began stroking my shaft against her wetness. I got hard as shit. She grimaced as she slowly eased down on my rod. As soon as she adjusted to my size, the phone started ringing. I saw that it was Adonis, but I was enjoying what Kay Kay was doing so I ignored the phone call.

"Sshit!" I hissed as Kay Kay rocked her hips back and forth, speeding up her pace.

The headboard was hitting against the wall. I grabbed her waist and slowly slid her up and down my pole.

The phone started ringing again.

"MAN, FUCK!" I shouted, reaching for the phone to answer it.

Kay Kay didn't give a fuck about Adonis calling back, she was in a zone. Her eyes were rolling in her head.

"AAAH shit!" she moaned, throwing her head back.

The phone was still ringing in my hand.

"Just answer the damn phone," she breathed, still keeping her pace.

"Yeah," I answered in a strangled voice, tryna talk while Kay Kay was bouncing up and down on my dick.

"Nigga, meet me at Virgo Lounge, we need to talk," he said.

"When?" I grunted, tryna hide the fact that I was 'bout to bust a nut.

"Now, muthafucka, and tell Kay Kay to hurry up and crack that nut, fuck boy." He ended the call.

I'd let Kay Kay have the advantage long enough. I grabbed her by her shoulders and pulled her all the way down. I held her in place as I thrusted deep inside her. She planted her hands on my chest for balance. I gripped that fat ass of hers and bounced her up and down as I thrusted deeply.

"OOOH SHIT!" Her body jerked, and I felt her nut running down my dick; that made me cum.

***

"Damn, nigga, this place lit as fuck," I commended, looking around at the renovations that were almost complete.

"Yeah, they hookin' this shit up," Adonis said proudly, as he gave me dap.

Grabbing a bottle of 1738, we headed to the back office. He grabbed some ice outta the mini fridge, then poured us each a glass.

"First, congratulations. My nigga 'bout to be a daddy," he beamed, raising his glass to mine.

I thanked him.

"You my nigga and all, but next time I call and you fuckin', nigga, don't answer the fuckin' phone," he laughed.

"Nigga, you called back to back like you a bitch or something. I thought the shit was important," I replied sitting on the chair across from his desk.

"It is important." His tone got serious as he sat at his desk.

"I talked to Beans," he said, reaching in his desk and pulling out a small piece of paper. He passed it to me.

"Who's Ashley Brooks?" I asked, baffled.

"That's the bitch who has my baby," he stated.

"Oh, so we handling this shit?" I was ready to put in work and bring my niece home where she belongs.

"Beans gon' call me with some info on her schedule," he told me.

He poured another glass of 1738.

"Me and Venus getting married soon," he beamed.

"What's soon, nigga?" I asked.

"As soon as she can get shit together. I ain't with no wedding planning shit. Just let me pick my tux, and tell me when, where, and what time to show up," he chuckled.

"I hear that shit; bitches be wanting our opinions on too much shit. I don't give a fuck about no flowers and shit," I laughed.

Adonis's phone started ringing.

"Shit, that's Beans now," he said before answering.

"WHAT!" he shouted. "Beans, how the fuck you find that out?" he questioned.

The tone of his voice let me know that Beans just gave him some real fucked ass information.

"Aight, thanks, Beans." He ended the call.

"THAT BITCH!" he screamed throwing his glass at the wall.

"What the hell was that about?" I inquired.

His chest was rising and falling rapidly, as he paced back and forth with his head held down, pinching the bridge of his nose.

"I swear when I get to that bitch, I'm gon' kill her with my bare hands. She gon' wish she never met me. She got the muthafuckin' balls to kidnap my daughter. MY DAUGHTER LIKE SHE DON'T KNOW WHO FUCK I AM." He swiped his arms across his desk sending everything crashing to the floor.

"Yo, nigga, chill! Sit down and tell me what the fuck Beans just said." I was concerned.

Whatever Beans told that nigga had his ass on a thousand right now.

"Loco, we handling this shit tonight. I want this bitch found now. Whoever Ashley is, she better tell me what the fuck I wanna know or that bitch gon' die a slow painful death," he raged.

I let him rant, before trying to get the information out of him. He grabbed another glass and poured another drink.

"That bitch is gon' pay." He bounced his knee up and down.

I knew some shit was about to go down. I called Kay Kay to tell her that I wasn't gon' make dinner tonight and to cancel the reservations.

"What's going on? Why you can't make it?" she questioned.

"I got shit to do." She knows I don't tell her shit I got to do in the streets.

"Ok. Well, I'm with Venus anyway, so I'll just take her," she replied.

"Aight, call you later," I told her.

"Loco?" She called my name in a low voice. I already knew what was coming next.

"Be safe. I love you," she stated.

"Always, baby, love you too." She stayed tryna make a nigga say the 'L' word.

I have to stop this shit soon, I thought. Not only does it worry the fuck outta Kay Kay, but I'm about to have a son and it ain't no way my lil' soldier gon' be in the fuckin' streets. He gon' be in them books, going to college and shit. I want him to know that it's other ways to get bread instead of hustlin' and playing ball. I mean, shit, if the nigga got the talent to be a baller, that's cool. But he ain't never going into this lifestyle. Fuck that.

Adonis was sitting at the desk silent, blankly staring at the wall, tight faced with furrowed brows. This nigga was heated and the dark look in his eye said that he was out for blood. At this point, ain't nobody safe.

"Let's go, nigga. We got some shit to handle right now," he spoke calmly, as he grabbed the piece of paper and headed out the door.

I grabbed my phone off the desk and followed him out the door. It was time to do what we had to do.

"So this just some random kidnapping? This bitch doesn't look like she's into no street shit," I wondered, looking at Ashley's picture.

She was a beautiful, brown-skinned lady with big doe eyes, long straight hair, and she was wearing glasses. Now I'm no fool, I know looks can be deceiving, but this bitch looked like a fuckin' nerd.

"Naw, this shit wasn't random, and I know who she's connected to. I just don't know how, but I promise the bitch gon' wish she never fucked with me," he replied.

He still didn't tell me who the fuck the bitch was, but I let that shit go. He would tell me whenever he wants. From now, I'ma just do what the fuck I got to do tonight to make sure we get the information we need from this Ashley bitch.

Adonis

"That bitch is connected to the kidnapper." Beans's words were running a marathon in my mind, and I couldn't get the shit out. For a while now, I've been in battle with myself wondering if all this was behind some shit I did. I would ask myself that question, then try to convince myself that it wasn't. Beans just confirmed the answer to that question, this is my fuckin' fault.

I ran my hands down my face, letting out a loud sigh. Loco looked over at me.

"So you gon' tell me what the fuck's going on or what?" he inquired.

I know I got to tell this nigga, but admitting that my baby is missing 'cause of some shit I did, is hard to do. Knowing Loco like I do, he won't judge me. I, on the other hand, am judging myself. I made some stupid ass choices in life, and they put my family in danger. *Lavelle don't be disappointed in me. I understand now street life and home life should never mix, and I brought the streets into my home and let the bitch get comfortable. I promise though, once I handle this situation, I'm out. Fuck this life. The longer I stay, the deeper into it I get, and I know that the only way out would be jail or death. I don't choose either one of those muthafuckas. I refuse to put Venus in any more pain than I already have. Shit, look where this life put you and you ain't make no dumb ass decisions like me.* I was thinking and talking to my brother silently.

"Yo, you aight, nigga?" Loco asked as he glanced over at me.

"Yeah, nigga. Beans told me that Brooks is Ashley's married name. Her maiden name is Martin," I told him.

"Are you serious right now?" he questioned with a perplexed look.

"Dead ass," I answered.

We pulled into the warehouse where we keep our shit. We got out of the car and headed inside.

"What's up, Smoke?" Loco spoke, giving Smoke dap.

"What's up?" he replied then spoke and gave me dap.

We ain't have time for all the pleasantries, we were here to get suited. We got to get that bitch Ashley tonight. After Beans's phone call, I had more questions than I had answers to, and that bitch better give them to me.

We arrived at the address I had written on the sheet of paper. Loco got out first and checked shit out for us. I sat in the car, trying to be as patient as I could, but knowing that my child might be in that house had me wanting to just go kick the door in and claim what's mine. Loco came back to the car.

"Yo, the house is quiet. It's just a nigga in there watching TV in the living room," he informed me.

"So that bitch ain't in there with my baby?" I asked.

"I only can see what's downstairs. We blinded by what's upstairs so we have to be cautious as always, nigga. Don't let this shit get in yo' head. You know how we do. Now, let's get in here and find yo' baby," he instructed.

Usually I'm the one giving orders, but he was right. I can't let this shit fuck up my head. I nodded my head in agreement and took a few breaths to calm my nerves. We got outta the car and made our way to the house.

"There's a way in the house through the basement. I think we should go in that way and creep up on the nigga," Loco suggested.

"Ok, let's do it." I agreed.

Loco found an unlocked window, and he climbed in it. He carefully opened the door and me and Smoke quietly walked inside. With our guns loaded and cocked, we crept up the carpeted basement steps. Once out of the basement, I went to the right and Loco and Smoke went to the left. I crept up on the nigga.

"What the fuck?" he shouted as he jumped up on the sofa.

"Where's Ashley?" I asked in a sinister voice.

"I... I... I don't know where she is," he stuttered.

Loco put him in a chokehold from behind, while Smoke pressed his pistol against his temple.

"Nigga, if you want to live, you will tell me where the fuck yo' wife is with my fuckin' daughter," I stated as I placed my gun on the nigga's knee.

"I don't know; I haven't seen or heard from Ashley since she left me," he replied in a tremulous voice.

PEW!

"AAAAHH FUCK!" he shouted. I shot him in the knee.

"This is her address, so don't FUCKIN' LIE TO ME!" I warned him.

PEW!

I shot him in the other knee just to make sure he got the message.

His breathing was rapid, and fear was shown in his eyes. His sweaty body was shaking from pain mixed with fear.

WACK! WACK! WACK!

I punched him three times in the face with my brass knuckles on, cutting his face.

"Look, I can show you. Ashley left me months ago when her sister showed up here. She told me it was over, and took off. She hasn't been back since. I don't know where she is, I swear." He was talking fast as shit. "Look in my phone. I got a message from her telling me to file for divorce 'cause she ain't coming back. It was four months ago."

"Who's her sister?" I asked as Smoke grabbed the nigga's phone off the table.

"Alexia," he replied.

"Alexia Martin?" I asked, confirming their connection.

"Yeah, that's her sister. She's a crazy ass bitch and she's into some heavy shit," he stated.

I was mad as hell. That bitch stays fuckin' up my life, but this time it's gon' cost her; she will pay with her life.

"I SHOULD'VE KILLED THAT BITCH!" I yelled, pissed with myself.

Only reason why the bitch still living is 'cause she was pregnant, and I would never harm a child.

"What's the password to the phone?" Smoke asked.

"It's 162802," he called out.

Smoke put in the password and showed me the message. He was telling the truth. I tried to call the number from his phone, but it was no longer in service.

"I'm telling the truth; I haven't seen or heard from her since," he spoke in a pleading voice.

"Ok." I put his phone in my pocket and my gun in the small of my back. "Aight, y'all, he's telling the truth. Let's go." I turned on my heels and walked away.

Loco tightened his grip around the nigga's throat, and strangled him to death.

"Nigga, you had to do it the hard way?" I asked, chuckling.

"Man, it's been a long time since I choked a nigga out," he replied.

I called Roland, the head of the cleaning crew, and gave him the address to where we were. Once they arrived, we left.

My blood was boiling the whole ride back to the warehouse. I knew for sure we were gon' get that bitch and get my baby back tonight. Sitting at the table in the warehouse thinking about Raquel, Alexia, or whatever the fuck her name is, being behind this shit, got me fucked up. It seems like that bitch is always one step ahead of us.

"SHIT!" I shouted as I flipped over the table. "How the fuck am I gon' tell Venus this shit?" I blurted.

"Nigga, you don't. When we get the baby back, she ain't gon' give a fuck about nothing else," Loco advised.

"Yeah, you right. We gon' find that bitch and this time, she gon' die and that bastard child of hers will be an orphan," I spoke truthfully.

I don't give a fuck about shit but getting my daughter from that bitch. I swear if any harm is done to my child, I'm gon' make her death extremely painful and extremely slow.

"What's next?" Loco asked.

"I'm going to go see Beans, he needs to find this bitch NOW. We know them bitches' connection, so we'll probably find them together," I answered.

We finished doing what we had to do at the warehouse, then I called Beans and told him I was coming to see him.

***

"Beans, the bitch don't live there no more. Her husband said she left him months ago," I told him, sitting at his workstation.

"I told you give me a few days to tail her, nigga, you jumped the gun," he stated.

"Yeah, but when you said she was connected to that bitch Alexia, I was so pissed I had to go," I explained.

"You could've told me, then I would've told you to get out yo' got damn feelings and use yo' fucking head," he barked.

"Well, Alexia is that bitch's sister, so find her," I commanded.

"I will. It might take some time since this is the only information I have. But I can find her, no problem with that," he assured.

After giving him Ashley's husband wallet and phone and promising that I would wait until he actually finds this bitch before doing anything else, I headed home. I drove in silence tryna figure out what could I to do to keep my mind off of the situation. I decided that I would try to put my focus on getting the clubs opened and getting married, and leave finding Ashley and Alexia to Beans. Shit, I was already mentally drained. As soon as I walked into the bedroom, Venus started running her got damn mouth, going on and on about the wedding.

"Oh my goodness, Adonis, we can have our wedding at the place we wanted! Only thing is it would have to be in a month 'cause they booked for the next few months after that, but I don't think that should be a problem. I saw the perfect dress in this dress shop a while ago, I just have to go for a fitting, and we don't have many people that we are inviting so the guest list ain't gonna be no problem, and decorations, me and Kay Kay can pick those out. Do you want to go cake tasting with me? You really don't have to, I know what you like. Oh, and I found a place to get your tux from." Venus was excitedly rambling on and on about this wedding, making my head spin. I don't know what the hell happened in a day, but her and Kay Kay were already getting shit done.

"Whatever you want, baby. It's cool," I responded as I laid my head on the pillow.

She picked up the phone and called Kay Kay and hit the speaker button.

"Hey, Adonis is cool with it being next month, so I will call in the morning and we can go pay them," she spoke into the phone.

My head already was spinning and I really didn't want to hear them going on and on about the details. Kay Kay's voice was blaring through the speaker; she was being all loud and extra. I couldn't hear my own self think. I could hear Loco in the background telling her to shut her loud ass up. I laughed to myself. I covered my head with my pillow and let out a loud sigh.

"I'm getting on your nerves?" Venus asked, removing the pillow from my head.

Hell yeah, I thought, but I answered, "I'm about to go shower, so you got 20 minutes left to run yo' fuckin' mouth cause when I get out, I need to relieve some stress."

"Adonis, we already slipped up once, I'm still not healed all the way," she said, thinking I was gonna pay attention to anything she was saying.

I ignored her. I ain't tryna hear all that we can't fuck shit. I'm gon' go shower, fuck the shit outta her, and fuck up some of that food she cooked.

"Oh, Adonis, do you care about the colors of the wedding?" she yelled as I was closing the bathroom door.

"I don't give a fuck, long as I'm wearing black," I shouted.

I was already tired of wedding shit; bitches be driving a muthafucka crazy. They want our input on every fuckin' thing. When are they gon' realize we simple muthafuckas, and we want simple shit.

"Damn, I'll be glad when this wedding is over," I whispered as the hot water from the shower cascaded down my back.

Havoc

We finally got everything we need to go handle these D.C. niggas. Ash came through as usual. She sent this bitch here and she getting on my fucking nerves, keep talkin' some crazy shit about her baby dead and shit. I don't know what the fuck the bitch is talkin' 'bout and I don't give a fuck. All I want to do is go handle these muthafuckas and get back on my grind.

"Havoc, Ash want you," Alexia said in a flat voice. She tossed me my phone and left out the door.

Crazy bitch, I thought as I answered the phone.

"Yo, what the fuck wrong with yo' sister? Her ass walkin' around here looking spaced out and shit. Only time she seems normal is when she's talkin' to her baby, and why the fuck she keep on talkin' 'bout a dead ass baby for?" I inquired.

"She's suffering right now, but she'll be fine. Just handle these niggas and I'll come back with y'all to take care of my sister," she stated.

"Aight, cool."

"What's going on with your team?"

"Most of them out, they couldn't wait. I'm down to five now, but we got this."

"You better 'cause if you fuck up, they gon' kill us all."

"We got this, just call when we need to come." Ashley ended the call.

"You sure we can do this with just us five?" Junior asked.

"We can," I answered. "We gon' hit them niggas on their turf and take their shit."

"I'm down with that, I'm just ready to get my shit right." Floyd shook his head. "A nigga is broke as fuck right now. I can't live like this."

"Don't worry, Ash said they not checkin' for us so we can hit them when they least expect it," I told him.

The wedding day

Adonis

Today I'm marrying my best friend, my kids' mother, my everything. I should be filled with happiness, but I'm not. A sadness is present inside of me. Serene should be here watching her parents confess their love in front of friends, family, and God himself. But instead, she's with some crazy bitch who's obsessed with getting revenge on me. For what? 'Cause a nigga didn't want her. This shit wild. How the fuck she gon' have so much hatred toward me when her hoe ass was tryna play my ass in the first place. She chose to act like we were something we were not. Why? 'Cause I took the bitch out to eat sometimes, let her stay with me. She didn't have nowhere to go so fuck it; she was giving up the pussy and I was taking it, point blank. I leaned my head back on the sofa as thoughts of my baby ran through my mind. I promise if she harms my baby, she gon' regret the day she was born. The bitch probably already regrets that. Shit, her mother should've swallowed her ass.

"Aye, nigga, why you sitting over here looking all miserable and shit? You about to marry Venus, nigga. Ain't that what you wanted?" He sat down on the bench beside me.

"That's it, I'm marrying Venus and our daughter should be here. Muthafuckin' Beans can't find shit, and he been at this shit for a while," I snapped.

"Yeah man, I know. These bitches can pull a hell of a disappearing act. I got my nigga looking into it and he can't come up with shit," he informed me.

"Shit, nigga, this shit is mind boggling." I rubbed my hands across my head.

"Yeah, but they can't hide for too long. I want my niece back and them bitches dead, straight like that," he expressed.

"You know, man, Loco, you been through a lot with me lately, and I only hired you to be my hitta. It wasn't supposed to be like this," I stated, as I sat up on the bench and rested my elbows on my knees.

"Nigga, look, we fam. Point blank period. If you not good, I'm not good. We in this shit together." He gave me dap then pound his fist against his chest. I snickered.

"Lavelle not here, but he's smiling down on you. You really stepped up and became a man." He spoke in a serious tone.

"Yeah, well a man would have brought his baby home by now," I told him in a low tone.

"A man would walk through fire to bring his daughter home, you doing that." He stood. "Fuck all that shit, nigga, and get yo' ass off that fuckin' bench and finish getting ready. Fuck it, enjoy yo' day," he stressed.

"You better stop all that cursing in church," I chuckled as I stood up.

"Nigga, God knows my mouth." He put on his jacket and walked over to the mirror. "Nigga, why in the fuck am I so got damn nervous? It's yo' fuckin' wedding, not mine," Loco chuckled, adjusting the sleeves on the jacket to his Tom Ford tuxedo.

"Nigga, yo' ass nervous 'cause you think Kay Kay crazy ass gon' get wedding fever," I chuckled.

"Fuck that, you won't see me tying no knot no time soon." He was dead ass, and the frightened look on his face had us all cracking up.

"Yo, these tuxedos are the shit," Loco expressed, tucking the silver necktie. "Damn, it should be a muthafuckin' crime for a nigga to be so fuckin' fine. Now I know why I'm yo' best man," he added, admiring himself in the mirror.

"Ok, Mr. G.Q., this is my day not yours." I shook my head.

"Man, how in the hell you so damn calm right now?" Smoke asked, as he wiped away the tiny sweat beads that formed on the top of his nose.

"Because I love her and I been waiting on this day damn near my whole life," I replied.

"That's what's up," Daquan said, nodding his head.

"Man, cut all this sappy shit out. Save that shit for standing at the muthafuckin' altar," Loco blurted.

"What the fuck wrong with sappy shit? I tell my girl shit like that just to make her smile." Daquan shrugged his shoulders.

"That's 'cause she has yo' ass whipped," I tittered, slapping him on the shoulder.

Loco laughed and made the whipping motion

and sound.

"Y'all know this lil' nigga still wet behind the ears." Smoke laughed. "His ass gon' learn, the only reason to be sappy is to get the pussy; once you get it, keep that sappy shit to yo' got damn self. Real niggas don't do that shit," he added.

"Yeah, but a real man does." He got Smoke together real quick. Me and Loco was cracking the fuck up. "Y'all niggas over there laughing and shit, but y'all do the same shit. Adonis, especially you, over there laughing and shit. I know you always say that type of shit to my sister. And Loco, Kay Kay have yo' ass on lock, so fuck what y'all talkin' 'bout, I do what I do to keep my girl happy." He called himself putting us in our place.

We burst out laughing. My stomach muscles were starting to hurt. I needed that laugh.

"Boy, you better stop cursing at us before we put yo' lil ass in a circle," I chuckled.

This lil' nigga was real live pouting like a lil' ass boy. I was laughing so hard at his lil' young ass.

"Man, fuck y'all," he spat.

There was a knock at the door.

"Come in," I called out as I put on my jacket.

My mother walked in, looking gorgeous, in a long, silver, satin dress. I gave her a once over as I nodded my head in approval.

"You look beautiful, Ma," I complimented as she approached me.

She thanked me with a big grin on her face. She straightened my tie, then smoothed out the satin lapels on my jacket with tear filled eyes.

"You look so handsome," she sniffed, tryna hold back her tears. "Lavelle would've been so proud of you," she added. I wrapped my arms around her and held her tightly as she began to cry.

"Don't cry, Ma." I grabbed a tissue and dabbed away her tears, then kissed her cheek.

"This is an emotional day for me, for us both. It's bittersweet," she explained, referencing where we were standing.

Me and Venus decided to have our wedding at the same church we held Lavelle's funeral. She fell in love with the cathedral ceilings. At first, I felt uneasy about being in this church again. I thought it would've brought back the fucked up memories of that day. But actually, it felt like I was honoring him.

"You know your brother was hoping you got it together and do right by Venus, and today I feel like you're doing that, in spite of everything you're going through." I felt a lump form in my throat as I thought about my missing daughter.

"We're gonna get through this, Adonis. You're gonna bring Serene home safe and sound," she said as if she was reading my mind. She wiped away the tear that escaped my eye. "Enjoy today and worry about Serene tomorrow." She kissed then wiped her lipstick off my cheek.

She looked around the room at all the men with a look of pride on her face.

"All of y'all look so handsome today." She spoke in a brittle voice as she began tearing up again.

"Look, woman, stop all that crying. This is a happy day," Loco tittered, as he walked over to her and gave her a big hug.

"I can't help it, I'm so damn emotional right now," she giggled, pressing the corner of her eyes with the tissue.

"I've been waiting on the day to see my two handsome men get married since y'all were lil' knuckle heads running around, getting into trouble." She paused. "I would have loved to see Lavelle marry Sieda. I love that girl just like I love Venus." She started tearing up again.

"Here we go again," Loco snickered,

throwing his hands in the air.

"Loco, don't make me come over there," she threatened, giving him the evil eye.

"You got it, Ma. I ain't opening my mouth." He made the mouth zip and throw away the key gesture. I shook my head.

"Y'all some clowns, I swear," she snickered. She took a deep breath, then turned towards me and said, "It's about that time, baby. You ready?"

"You know I am," I replied, wrapping her arm around mine.

Venus

Harmony was sitting on the navy blue velvet sofa in the dressing room of the church, watching my hair get pinned up. My mother was helping Layna put on her dress, and Kay Kay was checking her makeup in the mirror.

"When can I put on my dress?" Harmony anxiously asked.

"In a few minutes. Just let me finish putting on my accessories and I'll help you," Sabrinae replied, as she put her earrings in her ear.

I glanced around the room, admiring how stunning everyone looked in their silver sleeveless bridesmaid's dresses. Sabrinae picked up the dress bag containing Harmony's dress.

"You ready to put this beautiful dress on?" she asked, unzipping the bag, revealing Harmony's dress.

Harmony quickly jumped off of the sofa, eager to put on her dress. We all laughed at her excitement. Sabrinae slowly slid Harmony into her dress, careful not to mess up her hair. Tears formed in my eyes. My baby girl looked so adorable. Ejoma, the stylist, stopped doing my makeup and dabbed away my tears.

"Mommy, do I look pretty?" Harmony asked, twirling around.

"Yes, you do, sweetheart," I replied.

Staring at Harmony twirling around, showing off her dress, I pictured my missing daughter dressed in a little dress matching Harmony's.

My heart began to feel heavy. I pray that whoever has her is taking care of her and not harming her in any way.

"I miss my daughter," I said in a low voice, as a tear rolled down my face.

Kay Kay placed her arm around my neck and laid her head on top of mine. My mother gently stroked my arms, trying to comfort me.

"Baby, please stop crying, I'm sure Adonis is doing everything he can to find her and bring her home safely."

"Yeah, Venus, stop crying. You supposed to be happy today." I could hear compassion in Layna's tone as she spoke in a softly spoken voice.

Ejoma blotted away the tear, then quickly applied a fresh coat of makeup. After spraying my face with a sealer, she turned me toward the mirror. I looked amazing.

"Come on, girl, let's hurry and get you in this dress," Kay Kay demanded as she grabbed my hand and pulled me out of the chair.

We hurried behind the curtain where I decided to get dressed. I didn't want anyone but my maid of honor, to see my dress until I had it on. Kay Kay was in awe as she unzipped the bag containing my dress; it was her first time seeing it.

"Oh my goodness, Venus, this is a really beautiful dress." She admired the stunning white Grecian styled mermaid dress, as she helped me slide into it.

I walked over to the full-length mirror to see how I looked. It fit me perfectly. I turned around to see the back and fell in love with the pearl beading that swirled from the front shoulder across my back. I twirled around, admiring myself from all angles. The light bouncing off the tiny specks of rhinestones that was placed over the sheer parts, made my dress sparkle with every turn.

Kay Kay snapped on the bow train with the pearl and rhinestone accentuating the center of the bow, and took a step back.

"Damn, girl, you look amazing," she spoke with admiration in her voice.

"Thanks, Kay Kay, and you look amazing

yourself," I said.

"I know. It's amazing how this dress hides my baby bump while still showing off my curves." She wiggled her hips from side to side, making me giggle.

She opened the curtain so I could reveal myself to everyone. My mother covered her opened mouth with her hands as her eyes started watering.

"You look so beautiful," she beamed, embracing me.

We stood in the middle of the dressing room, holding each other for a few minutes, while Kay Kay and the rest of the bridal party rushed out the door to go take their places at the altar. Adonis's mother came in the room wearing the same dress as my mom.

"It's time," she announced. "And you are the most beautiful bride I've ever seen," she added as she gave me a hug.

She passed Harmony the basket that held the white rose petals, then grabbed her hand and led her out the door. My mother wrapped her arm around mine.

"Let's go get you married," she said proudly, as she passed me my bouquet.

The intro music to "You and Me" by Johnny Gill started playing. Harmony walked in first, dropping the rose petals down the aisle, with her grandmothers following behind her. I wished I was already standing at the altar, watching my little girl walk down the aisle looking adorable in her dress.

I stood alone in the hallway behind the closed doors, anxiously waiting for the singer to start singing the lyrics to the song. I heard the preacher's voice over the music telling everybody to rise.

"Ok, Venus, get it together," I coached myself, trying to ignore the nervousness.

The doors opened and the singers started belting out the lyrics to the song, as I slowly walked down the aisle to join my husband to be.

It was time to say our vows. We chose not to write them, deciding to look into each other's eyes and speak from the heart.

"Venus, I promise to laugh with you, grow with you, always love you in good times as well as bad times. I promise to support you and share in your dreams as you achieve your goals. I promise to listen to you with understanding, and to always stand by your side as your best friend and partner, today and for the rest of our lives."

"Adonis, I choose you as my husband and best friend. I will always stand by your side and sleep in your arms. I promise to be the joy in your heart. I want to grow with you, to laugh with you, and to be the happiness in your times of struggles. If I had the choice to do it all over again, I'd choose you every time. I promise to work hard to make our now into our forever. I love you, Adonis, and I will choose you forever, through all eternity."

"I now pronounce you man and wife. You may now kiss your bride," the preacher announced. We kissed each other like we've never kissed before. In that moment, any doubts I've ever had about him disappeared. I was his and he was mine, forever.

Adonis

We decided to wait to go on a honeymoon 'cause of the situation with Serene. Beans could call at any time with the information I need, so I wanted to stay close to home. We went to Sofitel Washington D.C. Hotel in Lafayette Square. I got us the superior room, with a king size bed. I plan on using every inch of that bed tonight. Earlier, I came to the room to decorate it for my wife. I thought about how much she loved it when I had that romantic dinner for her. I wanted to mimic that idea. I had rose petals and candles placed around the room and on the bed, I made a beautiful heart made of roses with Mr. and Mrs. Thompson spelled out in the middle, with her favorite chocolate covered cherries. The kind with the clear liquid, not the creamy liquid. Chilling in the bucket was a bottle of limited edition Dom Perignon Rose.

We arrived at the hotel around 6 pm. I checked us in, then we went up to room. I had her wait in the hallway while I lit all the candles. When I came back, she was leaning against the wall with her arms folded.

"So you mad?" I asked, laughing.

"It's not funny," she pouted, as she tried to push past me.

I scooped her up in my arms. "I got to do this the right way, Mrs. Thompson." I carried her over the threshold.

Her eyes lit up when she saw the beautiful decorated room.

"You did this?" she questioned excitedly. I nodded my head.

I yoked her towards me and kissed her passionately. I kissed her neck as I picked her up, and she wrapped her legs around me. Not breaking our kiss, I walked her to the bedroom and put her down.

"Oh my God, Adonis, this is beautiful... and the heart on the bed. I love it." She was damn near in tears. "Mr. and Mrs. Thompson, I will never get tired of hearing that," she beamed.

I wrapped my arms around her waist and kissed the side of her neck. I picked up one of the candies and put it up to her mouth. She bit down, and the liquid ran down on her bottom lip. I licked it off.

"This dress is stunning as hell and as sexy as you look in it, I got to take it off of you." I kissed her again as I unzipped the dress.

I slid it down and she stepped out of it. I slid my hands up her leg as I stood back up.

"What we gonna do with all these chocolates?" she asked in a seductive voice.

"I'm sure we can be creative." I traced her mouth with my tongue as I stuck my hand in her panties.

"I brought some lingerie to wear for you tonight," she stated.

"Fuck that shit, I just want you ass naked." I slid her panties down and kissed her box. "This is officially mine now." I lifted her leg over my shoulder and gave it a nice kiss.

She pulled away and walked towards the bathroom. I knew she wanted to fuck in the shower, and I was happy to oblige. I took off my tux and followed her in to the bathroom.

"You lucky I don't care about getting my hair wet," she chirped, as the water flowed out of the rain shower head.

She stepped in the shower. I followed her, snatched her up into my arms, and kissed her. Backing her against the wall, I lifted her up. She wrapped her legs around my neck. I swirled my tongue around her pearl, inserting my fingers inside.

"MMMMM," she moaned loudly.

I glided my tongue up and down her clit, sucking and biting it lightly. I could feel her body shaking, as she let out loud screams of passion.

"Damn, you eating the shit outta me," she purred, throwing her head back.

"This my pussy," I mumbled as her body tensed around my neck.

She started panting as she grabbed on to my head and came in my mouth.

She slid down the wall.

I bent her over and pushed her against the wall, then smacked her on her apple rounded ass, leaving a red handprint.

"Ow, that shit hurt." She rubbed her ass.

I gripped her hips and slammed her back on my dick. I spread her ass cheeks so that I could see my dick go deep in and out of her. I thrusted in her so hard her body was slamming against the wall. I continued pounding her.

"Shit... Fuck... Got damn... Adonis!" She was shouting all types of shit as I made her cum. I thrusted hard and rough.

"Whose pussy is this?" I asked, ramming all 10 inches in one deep thrust.

"Yoouurs," she groaned.

"Who am I?" I grabbed the back of her hair, making her arch her back more.

"ADONIS!" she shouted.

"Wrong answer." I yanked her hair back harder as I plowed in her deeper, making my balls slap against her pussy.

"OOOOO GGGGOOODDDD!" she screamed. "You my husband," she breathed out, as she had another orgasm.

I rammed into her one last time, then I bust a nut on her ass, spreading her cheeks so I could watch it drip down her asshole. She was wobbling as if she was about to buckle.

"You know I'm not done with you yet." I picked her up and wrapped her legs around me.

I placed my arms around her waist and lifted her up and down on my pole. She leaned back, as I shifted my arms to support her in the air, then she put her legs around my shoulders. I grabbed her by the wrists and thrusted deeper. I backed her back against the wall, sliding her legs down my arms, opening her up wider. Gripping her waist, I pounded her hard and fast until she reached another orgasm.

We made our way out of the bathroom and in to the bedroom. I moved the chocolates off the bed, laid her in the middle of the heart of roses, then I placed a piece of the candy between her teeth and bit into it. As our tongues swirled around in each other's mouths, the sweet juice from the chocolate cherries ignited the fire that was burning in our bodies. I decided to use the candies in another way. I sucked, then bit down on the chocolate and traced around her nipples, letting it cover them with its sweetness. I lick, sucked, and nibbled on them, until her body started to quiver. I traced her body from between her chest to between her legs, leaving a trail of the sweet sticky juice, then I licked the juice off stopping her pussy.

Tasting the chocolate mixed with the taste of her box made me want to slurp the wetness even more. Gripping the sheets, she screamed in passion.

She was sliding up, tryna get away from my vicious attack on her pearl. I grabbed her hips and pulled her back. She wasn't getting away from me. I was hungry and I needed to eat my dessert. As I was devouring her pussy, I stuck a tiny piece of the chocolate in the tip of her asshole. I bit down on it and let the juice run down, before licking up and eating the candy out of the hole. She was squirming and moaning loudly, as my tongue gave her multiple orgasms. Her body still jerking and sensitive to my touch. I slid my rod up and down her clit, stuck the tip in and out of her in swift, quick motions. Just as she was about to cum, I rammed it inside with hard, deep thrusts.

"FUCK!" she blurted out as I hit her g-spot, making her body jerk like she was having a seizure.

We turned what started out as an all-night fuck session, into intimate lovemaking. It was slow, sensual, and full of passion, with our souls connecting as one.

Somewhere in DC......

"Aight, Havoc, I know exactly where them niggas gon' be at tonight. It's gonna be a little crowded but I know for a fact they gon' be unarmed. They with their bitches. We can take all of them out and get the fuck outta D.C. tonight," I told Havoc.

"What about their traps? We need to hit them up and get the products," he replied.

"Look, Havoc. The main thing tonight is to hit them. Once they are outta the picture, we can hit all the traps. My sister knows where they are," I explained. "Where the fuck is my sister anyway?" I asked.

"She stayed in Detroit. She didn't want them to find out she was here and get alarmed," he replied.

I picked up the phone and called Alexia, and she answered on the first ring.

"Is it done?" she questioned as soon as she answered the phone.

"It will be tonight, but without you, we can't hit the traps." I reminded her that we didn't know where their houses were.

"I'll text you the information. I can't risk being in D.C. Them niggas probably got eyes on me and if they find me there, then they gonna find you," she explained.

"Aight, Alexia. We gonna get this shit done and be home in the morning." I got off the phone with her.

A few minutes later, my phone pinged. Alexia texted me the addresses to their two major traps.

"Aight, she sent the addresses. We gone take these niggas out, swing pass the houses, change cars and get the fuck out. Got it?" I instructed.

"Yeah, we got it. My niggas are ready," Havoc assured.

"Hit me when it's done. I'll be ready when you get here," I said.

Saturday

Loco

"Kay Kay, hurry the hell up, they outside!" I yelled up the steps. I hate waiting for her to get dressed, she takes forever.

We're going to DC Improv Comedy Club and Restaurant with Adonis and Venus. It's open mic night. Me and Adonis like entertainers that are not well known. It's like we watch them build their career from the ground up. Like that underground type shit. Some of them muthafuckas be better than the big name artists.

"Ok, I'm ready," Kay Kay breathed out, coming down the steps. "This baby got me winded as shit," she added.

"That's just yo' laziness," I chuckled, as I wrapped my arms around her.

I rubbed on her protruding belly.

"My son gon' be perfect," I whispered, as I kissed her on her shoulder.

"I hope it's some funny comedians tonight," she said, grabbing her clutch.

We got in the car and Adonis immediately started talking shit.

"What the fuck took y'all asses so got dam long? I been out here for an hour. Shit, we gon' miss the show." Venus slapped him on the arm.

"Adonis, stop fuckin' with them. You know damn well we was not out here that long," she chuckled.

"Whatever. Kay Kay's ass thinks she's a fuckin' beauty queen," he teased.

"Nigga, please. I look better than them bitches," she giggled.

We talked shit to each other the whole entire ride to the comedy club. That's what we do though.

"Aye, Venus, how you deal with this stupid ass muthafucka every day?" I asked, playing.

"I know how to shut his ass up," she replied.

"Yeah, she put her pussy in my face. A nigga can't say shit with a mouthful of pussy," he laughed.

"Nasty ass." Venus slapped him in his head. We all started cracking up.

"Venus, he does have a point though. The only way to keep Kay Kay's ass quiet it to put dick in her mouth," I joked.

"Sho' is," Kay Kay agreed.

"You know what, y'all a bunch of perverts," Venus giggled then snorted.

It trips me out the way her and Harmony snort after they giggle.

We arrived at the comedy club and parked in our reserved spots in the parking garage and walked up to the club.

"Man, I can't wait to eat. My stomach on E right now." Adonis rubbed his stomach as he sat in the seat.

Venus opened the menu and started browsing it. We tried to order every fuckin' thing on the menu. Sliders, nachos, wings, potatoes skins, Quesadillas, and a bottle of Moet. We were being greedy as fuck.

The show was funny as hell. It's some real raw talent out there. Niggas and bitches straight from the audience was getting on that mic, cracking jokes like they were already pros. Adonis's goofy ass was laughing so hard at one of the niggas, he almost fell out of the chair.

After the show, we were standing out front talking about the show, enjoying the warm weather. I noticed a car speed up the street once. For some reason, something didn't feel right about that car.

"Aye, let's start walking to the car," I said, guiding Kay Kay and Venus in front of us.

"Loco, damn, why you rushing us? The damn garage is only a few feet away," Kay Kay complained 'cause I was pushing them.

"What's up?" Adonis mouthed noticing my demeanor.

Just I was 'bout to tell him, I noticed the car again, and something caught my attention. Guns was sticking out of the windows.

"GO!" I yelled pushing Kay Kay and Venus in the garage. Adonis turned around just as shots rang out.

POP! POP! POP! POP!

I grabbed him and threw him on the ground. The screeching of the tires let me know whoever they were sped away.

Venus and Kay Kay came rushing over to us.

"ADONIS!" Venus screamed noticing the blood all over his shirt.

"I'm ok," he said as she fell into his arms.

She started checking all over him, tryna see where he was shot at.

"NOOOOOO!" Kay Kay yelled as I hit the ground.

"Loco, don't you die, you hear me," she was crying.

The heat from the bullet in my chest was sending burning sensations through my body. I cringed as my body started shivering.

"Nigga, you ain't goin' out like this, hang in there," Adonis groaned, holding his arm.

I noticed that he was bleeding.

Kay Kay laid her head on top of mine and started praying as she held my hand tightly.

I heard sirens blaring from a distance as my eyes slowly closed.

Kay Kay

"Loco, baby, please don't close your eyes. Open them back up." Tears rolled down my face as I pleaded for him to stay awake. "Think about your son, he needs you." I wiped away the tears. "I need you," I whispered.

He squeezed my hand as I leaned over his motionless body. His chest was rising and falling rapidly as his breathing turned shallow. His body felt cold as beads of sweat formed on his skin. He opened his eyes, and his pupils were dilated. I felt his pulse weaken as I held on to his hand.

"No, don't close your eyes, look at me," I begged, as his eyes started to slowly close again.

"Miss, you have to clear the area," the paramedic said.

I didn't want to leave his side; my heart was breaking. Venus came over and wrapped her arms around me, pulling me away.

"Patient suffering from a gunshot wound in the anterior chest wall. He's going into hypovolemic shock," the other paramedic called out.

Placing Loco on the gurney, the paramedics moved quickly to try to stabilize him, before pulling away.

Adonis was on the sidewalk being treated for a gunshot wound to his arm. I noticed he had a distant look on his face and tears in his eyes.

"Is he alright?" I asked Venus.

"He's thinking about Lavelle," Venus apprised.

I wasn't thinking. Lavelle got shot in the chest and died in his arms.

"Oh my God, Loco," I cried out as reality hit me. Loco might actually die.

I started to feel light headed and hot. My chest started hurting and I could hardly breathe.

"Kay Kay, he's gonna be fine," she assured.

Adonis came over and told us that they were taking him to Washington Hospital Center. I called his mother on the way to the hospital, just in case the worst happens. The thought of losing him is unbearable.

"I don't know what I'll do if I lose him," I wept.

Adonis was silent, sitting in the passenger seat with his head rested on the headrest and hand on his head. Blood was seeping through his bandage.

"You gonna get that checked out, right?" Venus asked.

"I'm good, Venus. I gotta make sure he's ok," He snapped.

"Ok, but once we make sure he's ok, then you're getting your arm checked out," she demanded.

"Whatever," he replied.

I sat in the back seat sobbing, thinking about the way me and Loco bicker over small things.

I hope he makes it, I thought as I continued to sob.

We arrived at the hospital, and I rushed up to the information desk asking for information on Loco. All they could tell me was that he was in surgery. I sat in the chair in the waiting area, shaking. I was so scared.

Adonis sat beside me and placed his arm around my neck, and laid my head on his shoulder. He was in pain both physically and emotionally; it was written all over his face.

"Kay Kay," Mrs. Gaines called my name, rushing over to me. "Is he ok?" she asked with tear-filled eyes, as she threw her arms around me.

"I don't know, he's in surgery," I replied.

"Mrs. G, he'll pull through. You know it takes more than a bullet to stop yo' son," Adonis said as he gave her a hug.

"What about you? You look like you was hit too," she stated, noticing the bloody bandage on his arm.

"Yeah, the bullet went straight through, I'll be fine," he told her.

"He's gonna go get it looked at, Mrs. Gaines," Venus informed her.

An hour later, the surgeon came and informed us that Loco would be fine. The bullet didn't hit any major organs or arteries, and he's expected to make a full recovery.

"Thank God!" his mother shouted.

I was at a loss for words. The relief that washed over me was a welcoming feeling. Adonis walked over to me and gave me a hug.

"See, I told you it'll take more than a bullet to stop his crazy ass," he chuckled lightly.

"Now you, Adonis, get that arm looked at before Venus kills you," I replied.

"I'm going now. Plus, she's giving me a death stare right now. I feel her eyes burning through my back," he snickered.

***

We were all sitting in Loco's room, waiting for him to wake up. He was still sedated. I sat beside him, holding his hand and resting my head on the rail. It was hard to see him lying in that bed hooked to those machines.

"Baby, wake up so I'll know for sure you ok," I spoke in a small brittle voice.

"Kay Kay, he's fine. He'll wake up, I promise," his mother assured me, rubbing my shoulder.

Me and Venus were chatting with Mrs. Gaines, and Adonis was sitting in the chair on the other side of the room.

"Shit, what the fuck?" I heard Loco's groggy hoarse voice. "Damn," he groaned as he tried moving." I jumped out of my seat, ran over and threw my body over his.

"Fuck, Kay Kay," he grimaced.

"Oh, sorry," I apologized.

"I'm good," he groaned, as Adonis walked over to the bed.

Loco's mother hugged him from the other side of the bed.

"Damn, y'all tryna kill a nigga," he chuckled then grunted.

"Yeah, nigga, it was touch and go for a while. You flat lined twice. Yo' ass was almost gone." Adonis tried to sound serious as he walked over to the bed.

"Adonis, stop lying," I laughed.

"Nah, on some real shit, my nigga, you took a bullet for me. That's day one shit. Thanks," he said giving him dap.

"I told you before, we fam. We in this shit together," he reiterated.

The nurse came in and checked his vitals and gave him water. She left out of the room and looked over at Adonis. About an hour later, Loco's mother said that she had to go. She hadn't been feeling well lately so she needed to go home and rest. She leaned over Loco and kissed him on the cheek.

"You better not scare me like that no more, boy. You know you all I got." She kissed him again.

"I won't, Ma. Go home and get some rest." He kissed her hand.

"I'll call you and check on you when I leave here," I said as I gave her hug.

She hugged Adonis and Venus and left out the door. Loco watched as the door slowly closed behind her.

"Adonis—" he started.

"I already know, I'm on it. It ain't about to go down like that," Adonis said, cutting him off.

Loco motioned for me to sit beside him.

"You was scared, huh?" he asked, grabbing my hand.

"Hell yeah. I don't want to lose you, especially now that I'm having a baby," I replied, rubbing my belly.

"You tryna do this? You tryna be with a nigga forever?" he questioned.

I gave him a puzzled look.

"What the hell you think?" I cut my eyes at him.

"Aight, that's cool. I'll marry yo' crazy ass," he stated. I was confused.

"Nigga, I ain't ask you to marry me." I think his ass delusional or something.

"No, but I'm asking you. Marry me, Kaylee?" The seriousness in his tone matched the seriousness in his eyes.

"Ok, I will," I answered with a slight giggle, then leaned over and kissed him.

"Y'all and y'all proposals," Venus chuckled, rolling her neck and eyes, crossing her legs.

"What's wrong with our proposals?" Loco asked with furrowed brows.

Venus got up and stood next to Adonis. "This one proposed to me after he bust a nut, and you lying up in a hospital bed half dead. What happened to the romance? Getting down on one knee with flowers?"

"It's in the movies and on TV," Loco answered.

"Well, I want romance," she said, flopping back down in the chair.

"The wedding night, that's the romance," Adonis said. "Shiiid, first time you fuck knowing this officially yo' pussy, you dig all up in them guts," he added.

"Shiiid, Kay Kay already know about that long stroke," Loco chuckled then groaned.

Me and Venus both shook our heads. "This conversation is dead," I stated.

"How long they say a nigga got to be in here? I'm ready to leave," he asked.

"Your mother said the doctor said about a week or so," I told him.

We stayed for about another 20 minutes, then he told me to go home and get some rest. I was glad 'cause my back was hurting like shit.

I gave him a kiss. "Sweet dreams, my fiancé." I smiled then kissed him again.

"Goodnight," he whispered.

Adonis told Venus that he was dropping me off then her, 'cause he had to make a quick stop and that he would be home as soon as he finished.

"Adonis, please be careful," I pleaded.

"I'll be good, Kay Kay. Loco is fine, stop worrying."

He dropped me off and walked me to the door. He made sure I got in safely then he left.

Adonis

After being at the hospital all night, I was tired as hell and my arm was hurting like shit. But I had some shit to take care of and time was of the essence. I pulled up to Beans's spot. I knocked on the door and waited for him to unlock the million locks he had on the door.

"Yeah, nigga, what took you so fuckin' long?" I barked, walking in the door.

"You call me at the crack of dawn saying you on the way over. I had to get up and throw something on. Unless you wanted to see me in my boxers." He dragged his feet over to the workstation and sat down. "What you need?"

"Some niggas popped off on me and Loco last night. I took one in the arm but it went straight through. Loco laid in the hospital, he took a hit in the chest. That bullet was meant for me; I need to know who did it."

"I can tell you that right now." He logged on to his system. "I been keeping eyes on that bitch's credit card usage. I still haven't gotten her address but I see she left last night and stopped at the gas station a couple of times." He pointed to the screen showing me the locations of the gas station. "If I had to guess, I would say it was the niggas in Detroit. The bitch is going to Detroit, but let me sit on it for a few days just to be sure."

"Aight," I agreed.

This shit was starting to drive me crazy. I'm tired of running around all over the place tryna find these bitches. I just want the shit over with, get my child back, and open my fuckin' clubs. I can't keep doing this shit. I got too much to lose.

"I mean it this time. Adonis, give me a few days to make sure. You gotta let yo' arm heal anyway," he said.

"Nigga, they didn't hit my shooting arm. I'm good," I assured him. I gave him dap, then headed home to get some rest.

I replayed the scene from the shooting last night in my mind over and over. That shit was an eye opener for real. One minute we were talking and chilling, the next niggas were poppin' off on us. We all could've been dead. I can't keep putting my family's lives at risk. I promised that I'd get out when my mother was in the hospital, and I ain't lying. I been thinking about that shit a lot lately.

"I ain't doing shit until I get rid of all them muthafuckas in Detroit," I thought out loud.

If I was going to Detroit, I needed to get in and out undetected. I needed some heavy artillery. I picked up the phone and called the one muthafucka I know that can do both.

"Hola," he answered.

"Rojas, what's up?"

"Adonis, what's up?

"I need to meet with you."

"I'm at my home in New York. I can send my plane for you."

"How soon?"

"How's tomorrow?"

"Good for me."

"Ok, I'll see you tomorrow."

I'm glad that nigga isn't that far. Getting him to do what I need shouldn't be a problem, especially when he finds out my baby is missing.

When I got in the house, Venus and Harmony were cuddled in our bed, knocked out. I pictured Serene lying beside them. I closed my eyes and took a few breaths, tryna get my lil' princess outta my mind, but no matter how hard I tried, I couldn't. I have to find her.

I walked out of the room and went in to Serene's nursery. I grabbed her blanket and sat in the rocking chair, laying my head back as my heavy eyelids began to close.

The ringing phone awakened me. I looked at it and wondered what Rojas was calling me for. I let out a yawn and stretched as I answered the call.

"Adonis, what's up?" he asked loud as hell in my ear.

"Rojas, what the fuck you doing?" I responded.

"I'm at a club. Tomorrow we gon' partaaay. I gonna take you out, enjoy New York City, so be prepared. I fly you home after. Ok?" He sounded excited.

I really wasn't in the mood to go out partying, but I needed him to agree to do what I wanted him to do. I agreed to go out with him and we got off the phone. I went in the room, picked Harmony up and put her in her own bed. I took off my clothes and slid in bed and cuddled with Venus.

The next morning, I stepped in the shower thinking about all the shit I'd been dealing with. Leaving this shit behind has been weighing heavy on my mind, and I couldn't shake it. I never really worried so much about the danger I was putting my family in, but having this bitch come after my child directly, made me see that they were in more danger than I realized. It didn't have to be that bitch; it could've very well been a muthafucka that had beef with me or, was tryna get some money from me. Either way, I can't risk their lives anymore.

This better be my last muthafuckin' trip to Detroit, I thought. The steam from the hot shower made me feel relaxed. I leaned my head back and let the hot water stream down my face and my chest. I ran my hand across my face, clearing the water from my eyes.

"I need this shit handled now," I whispered to myself.

These niggas got a pass the first time and their asses couldn't live with that. Now they gotta die. That bitch, Ashley, gonna die as soon as she leads us to her sister. I should have never let that bitch in my fuckin' life. I took a deep breath, hoping to relieve some of my stress. I reached for the Dove men's soap and held it to my nose as I took a sniff. The fresh scent invaded my nostrils, giving me a calming feeling. I held it under the water, then started to lather up.

A sudden gush of cold air blew across my body, causing chills to run through me. I turned around and Venus was stepping in the shower.

"You want some company?" she asked, running her hands up my soapy chest.

She kneeled down to her knees, then slowly inserted my dick in her mouth. I let my head fall backward, enjoying the feeling of her warm mouth gliding up and down my shaft. I bit my bottom lip as she sucked a little tighter.

"SSSHIT!" I hissed looking down at her.

The water trickled in her soft curly hair, making it even curlier. I caressed her cheek. She looked up with those beautiful amber eyes of hers and connected with mine. With no words being said, we confessed our love. I knew from that moment that I was doing the right thing. Venus slid my pole in and out of her mouth, slowly taking all of it in. She swirled her tongue around the head, then slid it down my shaft and gently sucked the vein between my shaft and my balls. I gripped her hair.

"FUCK, VENUS!" I moaned. That shit felt good as fuck.

She sucked me back into her mouth, and sped up her pace. My knees started to feel weak.

"DAMN, BABY, SHIT!" I held on to the wall as I exploded in her mouth.

"Since you can't pick me up," she smirked, as she bent over grabbing her ankles.

I stroked my shaft to make it brick all the way up. I grabbed her hips and thrusted deep inside her roughly.

"AAAAHHH, ADONIS!" she shouted, as she grabbed the floor of the shower for support.

I sped up my stroke, plowing deeper into her. She let out a loud scream.

"What the fuck, Adonis, you trying to kill me?" she complained.

I slapped her on her ass, and the water splashed off of her making a loud smacking sound. She shrieked.

"ADONIS, STOP!" she shouted, rubbing the red handprint on her ass. I chuckled.

She started throwing her ass back, slamming it against me.

"Oh, you playing?" I gripped her by her waist and pulled her back into me.

"MMMM!" she moaned.

I'll admit I was playing with her lil' ass at first. I walked her over to the bench and put her leg up. I gripped her by her shoulders and pulled back. I pounded her hard and fast. She was panting, moaning, and screaming all types of curse words. I gripped her hair and pulled her head back.

"Don't ever think you gon' play sex games with me, I'll always win," I whispered in her ear as she let out a loud cry.

Her body shook violently, and her knees wobbled as she came. I thrusted in her a few good times, then exploded. My dick pulsating inside her made me wanna brick up again and go for another round.

****

"How long you gonna be in New York?" she asked, bent over, picking up the clothes I left on the closet floor.

"Just for the day. I have a little business to handle but I'll be back to give you some more dick," I replied, as I leaned over and kissed her.

"I didn't say I wanted more. I was just being nosy." She looked over her shoulder and smirked at me.

I smacked her on her ass. "It's not what you want, it's what you gon' get," I teased.

I continued getting dressed in my charcoal gray Armani suit. Venus placed the pile of clothes in the hamper, then walked over to me.

"I'm gonna miss you," she whined, fixing my collar.

"Yeah right. You probably gon' have that nigga up in my house while I'm gone. Tell him I said keep his ass off my side of the bed," I joked.

She playfully slapped me. "You tell those hoes in New York to keep their hands to themselves before I have to fuck me up a bitch." She got on her tiptoes and kissed me.

"See, I was being funny. Yo' lil violent ass had to get serious," I chuckled.

I scooped her in my arms, lifting her off the ground.

"Don't worry about no other bitch. You the only one I want." I kissed her passionately.

"Maybe I'll want some of that dick when you get home after all," she giggled.

I put her down, went to say goodbye to Harmony, then left for Regan National Airport.

Rojas's plane was already waiting when I arrived. Esteban, one of Rojas's security team, was waiting at the gate.

"Hey, Adonis, good to see you again," he greeted me, shaking my hand.

"What's up, Esteban? Good to see you as well," I responded.

We stepped on the plane. Rojas was sitting in a seat, smoking a Cohiba Behike cigar and drinking some whiskey.

"Adonis, come join me," he said, waving for me to sit with him. "Carmelita, bring Adonis a glass," he told his stewardess.

"Look at her, Adonis. She's a nice one that Carmelita," he chuckled, looking back at her ass.

He blew a kiss then he turned towards me. He offered me a cigar. I don't smoke but I took it, being courteous. Carmelita returned with my glass with two ice cubes in it.

"This is called Dalmore Selene. It's a 58-year-old whiskey, one of the finest in the world. It cost me around $30,000 a bottle," he boasted as he poured me a glass. "Salud," he toasted, lifting his glass.

"Salud," I replied, lifting my glass as well.

He reached over and lit my cigar for me. I took a small pull and damn near choked to death. Rojas laughed.

"Lighter, Adonis. You have to take it in slowly." He put his cigar to his mouth and took a pull, then blew out the smoke. "Go 'head, try it," he continued.

I placed the cigar in my mouth and followed his instructions. After about the third hit, I was lightheaded as fuck.

"How 'bout we talk business?" I suggested.

"Oh! My friend, Adonis, always a businessman first. That's why I like doing business with you. Ok, so let's talk business. What you need?" he asked, as he poured us another drink.

"I need a huge favor, and you'll be highly compensated for it," I told him.

"Ok, what's your favor?" he inquired, sitting back in his seat, crossing his legs.

I explained my situation to him and told him that I wanted to use his plane so I could get in and out of Detroit unnoticed.

"Adonis, I'm sorry your baby is missing. If it was my Maitea, I would be taking everybody's head, so of course I'll help. I give you anything you need. I'll send Esteban and Gael with the plane. No problem." He poured another drink and sat back in his seat with a distant look.

"Thank you, Rojas. I 'preciate it." I took another gulp of my drink.

By the time we reached JFK international airport, me and Rojas were both fucked up.

We got in his car and headed out of the airport.

"Tonight, Adonis, we going to Club Cache. It's Las Chicas Locas Sunday. We gonna do a little salsa dancing." He was moving in his seat like he was dancing.

I don't know shit about no damn salsa dancing. I shook my head. I was already feeling a little lightheaded from the drink and the cigar, and this nigga had some Spanish music blasting and he was singing loud and off key.

This is gonna be a long fuckin' night, I thought, as I laid my head back against the seat.

The sun was rising when I made it home. I was so fucked up; I was surprised I even made it in the house. I took off my shoes, shirt, and my jacket, and tossed them on the closet floor, stumbling like shit. Then I stepped outta my pants and staggered over to the bed and flopped down.

"Damn, Adonis, you wreak," Venus said with a groggy voice as she scrunched her face. "What the hell you been smoking?" she asked, covering her nose.

"Ro Ro Rojas had me sssmoking some damn beokie, behokie, behake, what the fuck everrr kind of cigars," I slurred.

I climbed in the bed and tried to wrap my arms around her.

"Boy, get off me, you stink." She pushed me away.

I didn't care, I just rolled back over and threw my arm around her. As soon as my head hit the pillow, I passed out.

Beans

It took me all night, but I was determined to find the correct address for Ashley Brooks. I went to the kitchen to get me another cup of coffee. When I got back to my workstation, I had a location. I finally had the correct address.

"I got you bitches now," I said to myself as I jotted down the information.

I turned my system off and went to get dressed. Being in my line of work, I was used to being up all night, so I decided to pay Ashley a little visit. I grabbed the paper containing her information and headed out the door.

When I arrived at her house, I saw a group of young niggas going in and out of her house with bags.

Those must be the young niggas that shot Adonis and Loco, I thought. I continued watching them to see what these young punks were up to.

"What the fuck are you niggas doing?" I whispered.

A few minutes later, Ashley emerged from the house carrying a purse and a suitcase.

"Where the fuck you think you going, Mrs. Brooks?" I said, as I watched Ashley and the niggas pile in to a minivan.

I jotted down the license plate number and ran it through my system. The car came back registered to Ashley. They pulled off and I decided to follow them. I stayed a few cars behind them to remain unnoticed. I followed them to 495 North headed towards Cabin John Parkway. I continued to follow them until they took I-270 North. I knew they were heading to Detroit so I continued to follow them a little while longer. As soon as they took I-70 West, I knew I was right. I took the next exit and headed back in the other direction, headed home. The sun was coming up and I felt that I had enough information to let Adonis know where they were headed. I decided to go home and take a little nap before calling Adonis with the information. I had to make sure I was fully alert if he needed anything. I decided to stay at my work spot so I could be near my system if I had to do any more work.

As soon as I got in, I lie in the bed and went right to sleep. I slept for a few hours. When I got up, I immediately called Adonis.

"Adonis, what's up?" I asked as soon as he answered the phone.

"What's up, Beans?" He sounded a little incoherent.

"Nigga, you been drinking this got damn early?" I asked.

"Naw, Beans. I'm still fucked up from last night's trip to NYC," he replied.

"You young boys can't hold yo' liquor. I tell you. Give me a bottle of moonshine and I'll show you how to drink, nigga," I laughed.

"Beans, ain't nobody fuckin' with yo' old ass," he chuckled. "What you calling me for, I know you ain't call just to fuck with a nigga?" he added.

"No, I found Ashley. She left in the wee hours of the morning with a car with about five young niggas with her. They headed for Detroit," I informed him.

"So we right, it was them bitches that hit us last night? Ok, no problems. I already planned for a road trip anyway. Thanks for the info," he said.

"Look, lay low for a few more days, let yo' arm get a little better. Let them think you don't know it was them. I'm gonna sit on the house for a few days to see if there's any activity, then I'll get back to you." He agreed then ended the call.

I went to my system and pulled up the database to see if I could hack into the traffic light cameras to see if I could find that minivan.

In Detroit...

My sister doesn't understand. She didn't have to do the things I did for money. She always had it. Her man was a businessman that had dealing in the streets. When he was killed, he left a shit load of money for her. She thought me selling my body for money was disgusting and disgraceful. Therefore, she basically disowned me. She's a stingy, hypocritical lil' bitch. She thinks I'm evil and twisted. I laugh at that. We were cut from the same cloth. She may not have been fuckin' for money like me, but she had a reputation of being a hoe. She had just as many dicks up in her as I have had. She doesn't even know who her son's father is. She thinks because she kept up with him all his life that she was a good and loving mother. She gave him up because she didn't want to be a single mother.

Havoc don't even know that Ashley's his mother. He just thinks that she's somebody that works with me and Maurice. He's the only reason she's helping me get revenge on Adonis and Venus. I told her that my man, Maurice, was looking to build his empire and we needed funding to get product. At first, she refused, but when I said he needed a team to help him take over Frank's shit, she agreed to give us funds we needed as well as send us to a connect that she knew. Her only request was that we put her son on. Maurice came up with this plan to get Havoc and his team started, then he would have what he needed to hire a team to take over Frank's empire. Adonis stopped that though.

When I got the package of Maurice's skinned off tattoo from Adonis, I had a nervous breakdown. I was scared because I knew then, he knew who I was and was coming for me. I called Ashley and she came to get me and helped me through my mental state. But that came with a cost. I asked her for a favor and she did it. Now she's using that favor against me to force me to help her son. But not anymore. I'm done with her shit.

I was sitting in the room when I heard all of them rushing in the house. Havoc was cursing. Apparently, they shot Adonis and Loco but they weren't dead. This shit doesn't make no fuckin' sense. These niggas running around here talkin' big shit like they hard but they couldn't take out two muthafuckas. On top of that, these niggas moved the traps so they couldn't get no shit. This is all fucked up. I was livid.

"YOU STUPID MUTHAFUCKAS, HOW IN THE HELL DID Y'ALL LET THEM LIVE?" I yelled at Havoc and his team. "Y'all had everything y'all needed to get them bitches and y'all bitches couldn't do that shit right. Adonis and his bitch should be dead. Fuck wrong with y'all bitch ass niggas?" I shook my head in disbelief.

"Yo, calm the fuck down, Alexia. Yo' crazy ass got one mo' time to come at me like I'm a fuck boy or somethin'," Havoc fumed.

"Fuckin' up the way you did, you is a fuck boy," I sneered. Havoc jumped up in my face like he was gonna hit me.

"Sit yo' monkey ass down, Havoc, my sister is right. All y'all niggas had to do was kill them muthafuckas and y'all couldn't do that. Actin' like you hard when you soft as a bitch," Ashley agreed.

"Now what? We didn't get to hit the traps and take their shit, and we didn't kill their asses." I was so mad I was seeing red. "Y'all fools don't get it. Those muthafuckas don't give a fuck, they gon' kill all of us." I took a deep breath. "Fuck y'all, I'm done. I'll handle shit for myself, no thanks to y'all dumb asses. I'll have my revenge, believe that." I cut my eyes at my sister.

I got to figure out something 'cause if Adonis knows about Ashley then he knows that she's my sister. Which means he knows everything and that means I'm dead. I was pissed the fuck off, I had to hit somebody.

SLAP!

I slapped Havoc with the back of my hand. He jumped up and grabbed me by the throat and stuck his gun in my mouth.

"You a crazy bitch! If you keep fuckin' with me and you won't have to worry about Adonis comin' for yo' ass 'cause I'ma blow yo' fuckin' brains out my got damn self." He pushed me away by my head. "Y'all bitches wanna blame us for this shit? Y'all brought us in to this. Now 'cause yo' nigga dead as fuck, and you want revenge and didn't get it, it's our fault. Fuck y'all simple bitches," Havoc snapped.

"Man, fuck all this; we need a plan. Them niggas sent our ass back to Detroit with our tails between our legs. Still broke," Ashley said as if she hurting for money.

"I think we need to find a connect and build our shit back up. Fuck the D.C. niggas. I'm out." Havoc got up and started to go upstairs.

"You can forget about him, but he would never forget about you. Your ass is dead," I laughed. "Dead man walking." I burst into laughter as he left the room.

He turned back around and said "Fuck you, your sister, and them niggas. Like I said, I'm out." He continued up the steps.

"Anybody else feels that way? Y'all niggas want out too?" Ashley questioned.

"We ride with Havoc, so whatever he do, we do." Floyd got up and walked out; the rest of the niggas followed.

"Fuck them, sis, we don't need them. We can do it by ourselves," Ashley tried convincing me.

"Yeah, but are we gon' live to do this shit? You don't know them niggas like I do. That muthafucka sent me my man's skinned off tattoo in a gift wrapped box. Like it was a present or something. What type of sick, twisted shit is that?" I explained, tryna get this bitch to understand the danger we're in. On top of all that, I got this nigga's baby.

"They got you this fuckin' shook, remember you owe me. I'm the one who got the baby for you. If I go down, you go down. So like it or not, you still in this," she snapped.

"I don't owe you shit. Like you said, if I go down, you down. And I have no intentions of going down. So if we gon' do this then I call the fuckin' shots from now on." I walked away.

Loco

"I have to get the fuck outta of this hospital, Kay Kay," I blurted out. I was already tired of being in the hospital and it's only been a few days. "Shit, I can check myself out and finish healing at home. It ain't like the shit was that fuckin' serious," I fumed.

"Orlando Tyrell Gaines, you are not checking yo' ass out of this hospital. The doctor said he will see you in a few more days and that's what the fuck's gonna happen," she retorted.

"Maaan, FUCK!" I shouted.

I was frustrated as hell. I felt a lot better. The pain wasn't as severe, plus, I wanted to get outta here so we could go handle them niggas in Detroit. Muthafuckas gon' try to roll up on us and try to take us out. That shit don't sit right with me.

"Loco, calm down. Damn, you gonna be out before you know it," she stated, browsing through her phone, shopping for baby shit.

I shook my head. "You thinking about baby shit, while I'm lying here pissed the fuck off," I snapped.

She got up and walk over to the bed, sitting down beside me.

"You know what you really need?" she asked as she slid her hand under the cover and started stroking my dick.

"MMMM!" I moaned lightly.

"Yeah, nigga, yo' ass stressed out 'cause you can't get a nut," she chuckled. "What the fuck you do when I wasn't talking to you?" she questioned.

"I suffered," I responded. "You know what works better, is if you put them sexy ass lips on it. Shiiid, yo' lips the reason why I have a newfound crush on Meagan Good," I joked.

"That's why yo' ass gonna stay sexually frustrated," she laughed, as she removed her hand off my dick.

She tried to get up but I pulled her back down and kissed her passionately.

"Come on, show yo' fiancé what that mouth do though." She bit down on her bottom lip, looking at me as if she was thinking about.

I started kissing on her neck. "You know you want to do it as much as I want you to," I mumbled into her neck.

She let out a low moan as she slid her hand back under my blanket.

"Aye, man, what the fuck is y'all muthafuckas in here tryna do? Fuck I walk in on?" Adonis's loud mouthed ass came busting in the room, running his mouth.

"Nigga, shut the fuck up," I sneered as I laid back on the pillow.

Kay Kay laughed. "That's what you get for being his friend." She cut her eyes at Adonis as she sat back in the chair.

"Shit, I'm starting to rethink this friendship," I said.

"Fuck you, nigga." Adonis acted like he was about to punch me in the chest.

I flinched. He was cracking up.

"I swear sometimes y'all act like lil' ass boys. I can't with y'all." Kay Kay shook her head.

Adonis sat down in the other chair and gave me a look. I knew he needed to tell me something.

"Kay Kay, go get something to eat. My son ain't had nothing in a while," I commanded.

She looked at me puzzled, but didn't say anything. She just grabbed her phone and her purse and left out the door.

"What's up?" I asked Adonis.

"Beans confirmed that it was the niggas from Detroit that hit us. He said that they are back in Detroit now, and check this shit out. That bitch Ashley is with them," he informed me.

"What? So them bitches working with them niggas? Oh, I have to get the fuck outta here. All their asses gon' be in the dirt ASAP," I raged.

"Hold on, nigga. I feel the same way, but Beans said that he wanted to sit on the bitch's house for a few days and he gon' call me and give me the green light. Plus, Rojas gon' fly us in and out with his plane. He gon' send Esteban and Gael with us so I need to let him know."

"Well, aight. By that time, my ass should be outta this bitch. If not, I'm checking myself the fuck out."

"Nigga, you think you gon' be able to handle this shit? You did just get shot in the chest," he reminded me.

"Muthafucka, didn't the doctor say it wasn't serious? I'm fine for real, for real. I got this. Yo' ass not handling this shit without me, you feel me?" I had to let him know I was dead ass.

"Aight, nigga, I feel that." He gave me dap. "I'ma be out; I'll tell Kay Kay come give you some top piece when I run into her," he laughed.

"Nigga, yo' ass always thinking freak type shit." I shook my head.

"So that's not what I walked in on?" He gave me a look that said he already knew the answer.

"Nigga, you don't know shit," I sneered.

"Please, 'cause if I was lying up in that bed right now, Venus's lil' ass would've had my dick all down her throat. Fuck that. I need some type of stress reliever, and on top of that, yo' weed head ass ain't smoke. Kay Kay's ass 'bout to get lock jaw fuckin' with you." I shook my head. That nigga was right. I gave him dap and he left.

Beans

For the last few days, I've been keeping a trace on the license plate number of the minivan Ashley and the young thugs drove off in. I see that they are in Detroit and haven't left. I decided to go to the house and take a look around to see if I can find anything of significance. Most of the time, there's always people out and about in the streets of D.C., so I had to wait a while to choose a good time to make my way into the house. So that I didn't look suspicious, I had my lock picking tool on a keychain. I picked the locks in no time flat. I stood in the middle of the foyer, looking around. The house was immaculate. I looked at the mail that was on the table by the door. I found bank statements, and credit card bills. I put those in my pocket. I walked around the house to see if I could notice anything out of place.

As I walked down the hallway, I noticed an office off the living room to the right. I went inside and started checking her computer. I couldn't crack the code so I had to hack into it another way. I pulled out my flash drive containing a program that overrides the password and allows access to the system. Once in her system, I pulled up her internet browser and checked her history.

"Ok, Ashley, now I see what you're up to," I said to myself.

Ashley had been searching how to kill someone using untraceable poison, home DNA testing, how to obtain a birth certificate and social security cards. She also was searching baby items. I exited her browser and checked her files on the computer.

You have it all planned out, I thought, reading the fake documents. A birth certificate with the name Maurizia Lewis. Mother's name Alexia Lewis and the father's name was Maurice Lewis. The other documents were a fake marriage license for Alexia and Maurice as well as forged hospital records. Alexia was planning to raise Serene as her own child. That only confirmed what I already thought, they were behind the attempt on Adonis's life. I saved the documents on my flash drive. I searched the drawers to see what else I could find.

The bottom drawer was locked so I picked it. I searched through the files. I got the deed to the house in D.C. and the house in Detroit. I made copies on her printer and put them in my pocket. Continuing my search through the files, I found a folder that looked like it was out of place. Everything else in the house was neatly put in its proper place except this particular folder. It looked as if she tried to stuff it in the back of the drawer. I opened the folder and there were pictures of Adonis's house that caught on fire, as well as pictures of Adonis and his family at various different places. But the one picture that stood out was a picture of the paid in advance ticket receipts for the comedy club from inside the office of his club. His club has been under renovations, so is somebody on the construction team working with them?

"The more I look in to this shit, the deeper it gets," I said, as I gathered the folder and headed out of the house.

I had everything that I needed to have to give Adonis the information he needed. He needed to take these people out 'cause they could be more dangerous than we thought. I got in my car and zoomed out of the neighborhood. I called Adonis on my way to my work spot.

"Come on, nigga, answer the fuckin' phone," I said as the phone continued to ring.

Just as I was about to hang up, I hear his voice.

"What's up, Beans?" he answered.

"I need you to meet me at my spot, now," I commanded.

With no questions asked, he agreed and was on his way.

Adonis arrived at my place a half an hour later. I let him in and went straight over to the workstation. I passed him the file that I took from Ashley's house and he opened it.

"What the fuck is this?" he asked, looking at the pictures of him and his family.

"I got that from Ashley's house. It seems that she's been watching you," I explained.

"So this bitch was tracking me?" he questioned.

"Yeah, she and them niggas from Detroit were working together. There's more," I told him as I pulled out the copies of the fake documents. "I found these documents as well. To me, it looks like Alexia was planning on raising Serene as her own child." I passed him the documents.

The veins in his forehead and neck started bulging.

"THIS BITCH REALLY THOUGHT I WOULD LET HER LIVE TO RAISE MY CHILD?" he yelled. "THIS BITCH MUST BE CRAZY IN HER FUCKIN' HEAD." He was enraged and I don't blame him.

"Adonis, I understand now how they seemed to avoid us. I got Ashley's bank statement and credit cards accounts. This bitch is loaded. She paid off people to do her dirty work and they did a damn good job." I briefed him on everything I found out.

"Well, I don't pay people to do my dirty work. I do the shit myself. All I need is the information. Tell me you got me information?" he replied.

I reached on the desk and gave him the paper containing the tag number to the vehicle along with the address to the house. He thanked me and hurried out of the door.

Adonis

After leaving Beans's spot, I knew what I needed to do. It was time to pay them Detroit muthafuckas a visit. I needed somebody to keep eyes on that house. The only person I could think about is the nigga Turk that L hooked me up with. I pulled out my phone and scrolled the contacts, hoping that I still had his number.

"Yes, I got that shit." I found his number.

I hit call and the phone started ringing. *Damn I hope the nigga remembers who I am*, I thought, as I impatiently waited for him to answer the phone.

"Who dis?" he answered.

"Aye, Turk, this Adonis. Loco introduced us a lil' while back. I got some ammo from you," I replied, explaining to the nigga who I was.

"Yeah, I remember, what's up?" he asked.

"I have a job for you, if you down. You'll be highly compensated," I stated.

"What you need?" he inquired.

"I need to handle some shit. I'll explain the situation when I get there, but I need eyes on a house in the Russell Woods on Tyler Street," I said.

"Over off Broadstreet Avenue, right?" he asked.

"Yeah," I answered.

He agreed to have eyes on the house. I told him that I needed a car and a hotel room. He told me that he would get whatever I needed. After discussing a time and place to meet, I ended the call with him and called Roland and let him know that I needed them to take a road trip. I wanted them to be in Detroit when I get there. I gave Roland detailed instructions on what I expected.

"I'll meet you before you leave with an envelope to give to Turk and another one for yo' team with a little extra for yo' expenses and travel.

"Aight, Adonis, I'll see you soon." We ended the call.

Last call I made was to Rojas to let him know when I needed the plane. He said he'll send everything I needed. We discussed the time and ended the conversation. It was time to put my plans in motion. I have everything needed in place. We're going to be in and out quickly and hopefully, bring my baby home.

I pulled out of Beans's place and headed home. I wanted to spend the evening with my family. With the life that I live, I spend a lot of time away from home and find myself having dinner alone. It will be nice to finally sit down and eat a home cooked meal with my family. I stopped at the florist and picked up a large bouquet of her favorite flowers in her favorite colors. Pink and purple roses and lilies. I had them placed in a large pink vase with a purple bow tied around it. The surrounding green leaves and the baby breath flowers were strategically placed throughout the bouquet, adding an extra touch to the bouquet. It was beautiful and I know my wife is gonna love it. I carefully placed the arrangement in the car and headed home.

Walking in the door, I noticed that the alarm didn't beep. I shook my head. This woman always forgets to keep the alarm on. I smelled food cooking and my stomach started growling. I placed the flowers down on the table and walked in the kitchen.

"What you cooking?" I asked, startling her.

"Oh my goodness, you scared me," she giggled, holding her chest. "I wasn't expecting you home so early," she said as she walked over to kiss me.

"I wanted to come home and sit down with my wife and child and have dinner." I wrapped my arms around her waist as she stirred the pot of linguini noodles.

"How many times do I have to tell you to keep the alarm on?" I asked as I planted soft kisses on her neck.

"Sorry, I forgot to activate it," she apologized, shrugging her shoulders.

I walked out of the kitchen and got the bouquet of flowers. I came back to the kitchen and set them on the counter.

"Oh my goodness, these are gorgeous," she exclaimed with a big grin on her face.

She thanked me and kissed me softly on the lips. "See how wonderful my husband is? He remembered all my favorites. What, you tryna get some tonight?" she tittered.

"I'm getting that anyway," I smirked, smacking her little round ass.

She went over to the counter and started chopping up vegetables for a salad. I washed my hands, grabbed a knife, and started helping her.

"Wow, what the hell is going on?" she questioned laughing. "Flowers and help with dinner. Ok, spill it. What the hell you do?" She placed her hand on her hips looking at me questionably.

"All I did was fall in love with a beautiful woman," I smiled, and blew her a kiss. "Venus, we gonna have more nights like this. I want to be more of a family," I explained.

"Wow, I'm really at a loss for words here," she beamed.

I leaned over and kissed her cheek. I put the vegetables that I cut in the bowl, then went over to the stove to see what she cooked. I removed the lid off of the skillet. I took a shrimp out and ate it.

"Shrimp scampi, huh?" I asked, munching on the shrimp.

"Keep yo' hand out of my food." She slapped my hand away from the pot.

I grabbed her up in my arms and kissed her.

"Eeeew, that's gross," Harmony said with her nose scrunched up.

We both looked at her surprised. How in the hell did she creep up on us? She usually makes her presence known the way she rips and runs around here.

The food was ready and we sat at the table as a family and ate. Harmony was running her mouth so much it was driving me and Venus crazy, but I loved every minute of it.

It's been awhile since we played together and I realized how much I missed hearing their laughter. Seeing my wife and daughter so happy was bittersweet for me. I wished Serene was here with us. I left the room for a brief moment to call Loco to tell him what the plans were for tomorrow night.

"You know I'm going, right?" he asked, but in reality he was telling me.

"Loco, you just got out—" I started to protest.

"I'm going, that's it and that's all," he cut me off. Then he hung up on me.

I didn't bother with calling him back. I already knew what the outcome would be. I sent him a quick text telling him what time I was picking him up, then I went back in the room and enjoyed my time with my family.

"This has been a great evening," Venus beamed, as she climbed on top of me.

"I see, you're glowing." I pulled one of her curls and let it go. I like to watch it spring back in place.

She leaned forward and kissed me. As our tongues flicked in and out of each other's mouth, I flipped her over.

"I love you," I said staring her in her eyes.

"I love you too," she replied, pulling me in for a kiss.

The next evening, I was in the closet preparing for my trip to Detroit. Venus was lying across the bed, gazing at me with a goofy ass grin on her face.

"What the hell you looking so fuckin' giddy about?" I asked, as I slid on my black pants.

"I was just thinking about last night," she giggled.

"Oh, you liked that, huh? What you like?" I question.

"How passionate and romantic you were when you made love to me," she beamed.

"Cut that soft shit out, just say you like how I fucked the shit outta of you." I walked over to her and kissed her forehead. "I probably got yo' ass pregnant all them seeds I shot in you," I chuckled.

"See, why are you turning something so sensual and beautiful into something so raunchy," she pouted, getting up from the bed.

"Why you gotta be all girly 'bout the shit?" I inquired.

"Y'all men get on my nerves. Why can't y'all just own up to your sensitive side?" She tried to walk past me but I caught her by her waist and wrapped my arms around her.

"What you want me to say, shit like our souls connected?" I kissed her on the nape of her neck. "Nah, I can't do that, but I can say my dick was sensitive as shit when I bust that third nut." She elbowed me in my stomach as I cracked up.

"You got problems," she said as she stormed into the bathroom.

I was laughing like shit while I finished getting dressed. She came outta the bathroom.

"I'm about to leave, I'll see you in a couple of hours." I kissed her. "When I get home, I'ma fuck all that soft shit outta you," I added.

She slapped me on the arm as I backed away from her. "Jerk," she called behind me.

I laughed and waved to her as I walked out the door.

I pulled into Loco's driveway. This nigga was already standing outside waiting for me. *This nigga fuckin' crazy as shit,* I thought as I shook my head. He came over to the car and got in.

"'Bout time you got here. A nigga been waitin' all fuckin' day," he sneered.

"Nigga, shut the fuck up. I told yo' ass what time I would be here. Nigga, I'm early," I tittered. "Man, for real, you good?" I asked, making sure he could do this.

"Yeah, muthafucka, I told you, I got this," he reiterated.

"Aight, nigga. If something happens to yo' ass, Kay Kay gon' kill you, not me," I said, pulling out of the driveway.

"Be real, she gon' kill both our asses with her evil ass," he laughed. "I would blame it on the pregnancy but her ass been fuckin' evil." He shook his head.

Loco been out of the hospital only a couple of days and this nigga already tryna put in work. I really wanted him to stay home and rest, but I knew that his ass was gon' be in Detroit whether he was on the plane with me or not.

"On some real shit, nigga, I hope we kill these muthafuckas and bring Serene home with ease. I can't keep doing this shit, not with lil' Orlando on the way. You know what I mean?" he said.

"Yeah, I do. Lavelle never wanted me in this fuckin' deep, but shit keeps happening, pulling me deeper and deeper into this shit," I stated.

"Fuck this shit. We sitting on stacks on top of stacks, we set for real, plus, we got the clubs to run. Let's handle this shit and be out," he suggested.

"I was thinking the same thing my nigga." I gave him dap.

The rest of the ride to the airport was silent. I was serious about giving all this shit up once I got my daughter. I think I will have that conversation with Rojas when I take him his plane back.

Earlier in Detroit...

I wasn't sticking around waiting for Adonis to come after me. Ashley is constantly reminding me that we are in this together and I can't leave. Fuck that! She can think that we safe all she wants, but I know the truth. Them niggas gon' come after us for sure and I can't be here when they do. Earlier today when they were out shopping for shit for the house, I took money out of my sister's room and packed me a bag. I had to get the hell out of Detroit, fast. I called an Uber and headed for the airport.

I was sitting in the Uber tryna decide what to do. I know I can't go too far into hiding right now, especially with this fuckin' crying ass baby. I looked over at her and she looked like she was about to start fussing again. *I know what I have to do,* I thought as the Uber came to a stop.

Sitting in the terminal of the airport, I searched my mind, thinking for a good place to go. As soon as I started to relax a little, Serene started fussing again. I picked her up.

"I wish you would just stop crying sometimes," I said as I gave her a bottle.

"Awww, how precious is she?" an older lady said, looking at Serene. "How old is she?" she asked.

"None of your fuckin' business," I replied as I got up and moved.

This shit is becoming too much for me. How am I gonna keep myself safe with a baby? I checked the flight schedule again and I made my decision. I know where I have to go to keep myself safe. I went up to the counter and purchased my ticket.

"Please sleep for the whole flight. You're stressing me the hell out," I whispered, rocking her to sleep.

We arrived at the airport, and I rented a car in one of my alias names. I put Serene in the car and headed to the hotel, hoping they would have a room available. I checked in my hotel, went in the room, and laid Serene on the bed. I sat down beside her, thinking of a way to make myself disappear. I came here for one reason and one reason only: to carry out my plans then leave. I took a quick shower and changed my clothes. I looked down at Serene shifting around and making grunting noises. I knew she was about to wake up. I shook as I rubbed my temples, tryna relieve a little bit of my stress.

First thing I have to do is get rid of this fuckin' baby. She's getting on my fuckin' nerves, always fuckin' crying and shit, I thought as I took a few deep breaths. I tried to care for her, but it's too much of a hassle. Plus, she fuckin' reminds me too much of Adonis and her eyes are the spitting image of that bitch. Serene shifted again and started wailing. I snapped.

"SHUT THE FUCK UP YOU FUCKIN' CRY BABY!" I shouted as I grabbed the pillow and placed it over her face.

"You want yo' momma? Is that it? That's why you always crying?" I pressed down on the pillow. "I hate that you love that bitch, I hate her, and I hate you," I spat holding the pillow tightly.

Suddenly, a calming feeling rushed over me, a feeling of peace. I knew what I was doing was wrong. Killing a baby was something I just couldn't do. I removed the pillow and Serene little body was still. *Please don't let it be too late,* I thought, hoping she was still alive. I picked her up and snuggled her against my chest. I placed her tiny body in a basket.

***

"I'm sorry, my sweet child, but you have to go away now. I wanted to raise you as my own, but I can't now. As much as mommy loves you, she hates you too." I planted a gentle kiss on her still body. "Don't worry my angel, you'll be in a better place."

"Dear God, watch over my baby, keep her safe and protected in your loving arms. In Jesus name I pray, Amen," I prayed for my baby.

With tear filled eyes, I kissed and grabbed her tiny hand. "Rest peacefully, my love." I kissed her fingers one last time before I walked away, heading to my destination.

Venus

"Isn't it a little too soon for you to be back working?" Pierre asked as he sat on the stool across from my drawing table.

"Hi, Pierre," I spoke. "I had to do something to keep my mind off of things." I shrugged my shoulders.

"Yeah, I understand. I'm sorry you going through that," he sympathized.

"Thank you, I appreciate that." He gave me a one arm hug.

"How's married life?" he asked.

"Boy, you know damn well you don't want to hear about my marriage," I chuckled, shaking my head.

He laughed. "Real talk, Venus, I just want you happy," he stated.

"I am," I responded with a smile.

We heard the door open, and Kay Kay came wobbling in, fumbling with her big ass purse. She made her way over to the table and flopped down in the chair beside me.

"Whew, girl. I don't know if this big ass baby boy knows it, but he makes it hard for me to fuckin' breathe. I be winded as shit," she huffed.

I laughed 'cause her baby is big and he's wearing her ass out. Loco think she's being lazy. He doesn't realize that his ass tall as fuck, and Kay Kay ain't too much bigger than me. She looks like she's having twins.

"What the hell you doing here anyway?" she asked, looking at me like I was crazy.

"I was working on some sketches on some new designs for a new line of maternity fashions," I answered.

"Oh wow!" she exclaimed.

"Yeah, as pregnant women, we struggle to stay fly. I know they made maternity wear a little more stylish, but I want to add a little more edge on it, make it more trendy. You know what I'm saying?"

Kay Kay rolled her chair closer so she could check out my sketches. I reached over and rubbed her belly and immediately started thinking about Serene. It really hurts that I can't hold her in my arms, feel her soft skin, or tell her I love her.

I felt Kay Kay wrap her arms around my neck, it was as if she was reading my mind.

I grabbed her arms and leaned in to her chest.

"I think this idea works. Let's do it and add it to the line we're preparing to show to buyers," she said, and Pierre agreed.

I continued sketching while Pierre and Kay Kay went through the menswear line. We decided to produce a few pieces from each line to show the potential buyers.

After work, I had to go to my mother's house to get Harmony. She was in the kitchen helping my mother and Layna cook dinner. I spoke to my mother and sister. Harmony asked if we could stay for dinner. I really didn't want to because I didn't know when Adonis was getting home and I wanted to be there when he got in. After begging and giving the sad face over and over, I agreed to stay.

I was sitting in the living room working on some more sketches, when Daquan came in and sat beside me.

"Aye sis, how you holdin' up?" he asked, pulling my head to his chest and kissing the top of my head. "Your lil' short ass," he chuckled.

"Boy, watch yo' mouth," I giggled, punching him in his arm. "I'm ok though," I answered, replying to his question.

My mother called us to the table for dinner. She blessed the food before we fixed our plates. As we sat and enjoyed our meal, I glanced at my mother and noticed how happy she looked. Then I thought about her story and a sense of pride washed over me. She's worked hard on her sobriety and has remained sober for the past three years. She hasn't had one relapse, even when she had to face her past by telling me her truth.

"Ma, I love you," I expressed. I don't know why, but at that moment I needed her to know that I loved her. After dinner, I helped my mother clean the dishes, then I headed home.

Adonis

Smoke was waiting for us in the parking lot when we pulled in to Reagan International. I shut the engine off and we got outta the car.

"What's up my nigga?" Smoke gave us both dap as he approached us.

"What's up, Smoke?" I spoke. "What's going on?" Inquired.

"I talked to Roland, they met with Turk. He said there's a car waiting for us at the airport. The keys are taped to it under the wheel. Turk left it for us," he informed.

"Aight, I'll hit 'em up when we land," I said.

We made our way to the plane. Esteban and Gael were waiting for us. We exchanged pleasantries then headed inside the plane to take our seats.

"Adonis, how are you?" Rojas spoke.

"Rojas, I didn't know you was coming," I replied. I was shocked he was there.

"I have to go home when you get back, so I decided to enjoy D.C. until you make it back. I have some gifts for you." He walked over to a trunk and opened it.

He had all types of assault rifles with silencers. Loco picked up an AR 15.

"You know this my wife right here," he said, holding it in the shooting position.

"Thanks, Rojas, good looking out." I gave him dap.

"Take care of your problem and I'll see you later." He nodded his head, then him and two of his other security men left the plane.

We took our seats and prepared for take-off. The flight was almost two hours long, so we discussed our plan. As always, Loco was gonna see who was inside and where they were at. Then we'd figure out the best way to enter. However, this time, I'm going through the front door with Esteban and Loco going through the back with Gael. Them niggas ain't gonna have no way out. We take out the niggas on the bottom, then clear out the upstairs. Only request I have is to leave that bitch Ashley alive so she can lead us to Alexia.

Like Smoke said, Turk had a car waiting for us when we stepped off the plane. We loaded up the ammo and headed to the address that Turk gave me to meet him at, which was right down the street from the niggas we were hittin'.

"Good to see you again, Turk," I said as I gave him dap.

I passed him the envelope containing $50,000. He thanked me then told me that he been keeping eyes on them and no one had come out of the house yet. I asked if he seen a baby with them.

"No, I just seen a bitch and five niggas," he told me.

He gave me another address to meet him at so he could get rid of the car. I told him that I would see him soon and left out.

We don't know Detroit like we know D.C., so we parked at the house but slightly out of sight. Loco got out and went to check shit out. Me and Esteban scanned the area to make sure no one was around, while Gael made sure we had an exit route. Loco got back to the car.

"These niggas like sitting ducks, they all chillin' in the front room, smoking weed and shit, waiting to die. The bitch, Ashley, in the kitchen look like she cleaning up. I say we go in like we planned in the plane. This should be quick and easy," he told us.

"Ok, let's go," I commanded.

Loco and Gael crept around the back, while me and Esteban crept to the front door. The burner phone flashed Loco's burner number, alerting me of the incoming call. I answered without saying a word. Loco pushed 1, then 2, then 3. We kicked both doors in at the same time. We entered with our guns already drawn.

"DON'T FUCKIN' MOVE!" I yelled as Loco and Gael came from the back with their guns drawn.

Loco had Ashley by her throat with one hand. He threw her on the ground at my feet. I placed my foot on her throat and pressed down. I wanted these niggas to know who we were, plus, I wanted to see the fear in these bitches' eyes as they knew they were about to die. I took my mask off, and so did Loco.

"Oh shit," the nigga I now know as Havoc said, as I gave him a death stare.

Esteban made sure the doors were closed, then him and Gael went to check the upstairs. They came back down to let me know that everything was clear. I nodded my head. We filled them niggas bodies with so many holes, blood was splashing all over the furniture and the walls.

Ashley was still under my foot tryna scream. I pressed down on her neck, cutting her air off. She squirmed, tryna free herself. I stood over top of her with a sinister smirk on my face.

"Do you know how much pleasure I would get from choking the life outta you right now?" I said through clenched teeth. "Get yo' muthafuckin' ass up," I demanded, snatching her up by her hair.

I grabbed her by the throat and slammed her into the wall.

"Please don't kill me," she cried.

"I'm not in the business of killing women," I lied.

I don't give a fuck who you are. You fucked with my child. You got to die.

"Where's Alexia?" I asked in a toneless voice.

"I... I... I don't know; she wasn't here when I got back this morning," she stuttered.

Slap!

"BITCH, DON'T FUCKIN' LIE TO ME!" I hollered in her face as I gripped her throat tighter.

I choked her until her face turned beet red and she looked like she was about to pass out.

I let her go. She slid on the floor crying and gasping for air. I picked her up by her throat again and slammed her back against the wall.

"I... I'm... not... lying," she spoke in a strangulated voice as she gasped for air.

I grabbed her, twisting her arm around her back and slammed her face first into the wall.

"AAAAAHHH!" She cried out in pain.

"If you don't tell me where the fuck your sister is I will break your fuckin' arm," I said as I applied pressure to her arm.

"Why did you help her steal my child?" I asked.

"She wanted revenge. She promised to help my son," she started crying.

I didn't have any pity on her. I applied more pressure to her arm. She cried out in pain.

"Talk. I don't give a fuck about yo' fuckin' tears," I stated coldly.

"She came to me after you killed Maurice. She had a miscarriage and was suffering a nervous breakdown. She thought that if she took your baby it would help her."

CRACK!

I broke her arm anyway. I don't give a fuck if Alexia lost her baby or if the bitch had a nervous breakdown. This bitch tried explaining that shit to me like she was justifying this bullshit.

She cried out in pain as she dropped to her knees. I picked her up by her hair and tossed her over to Esteban. He punched her in the face, then slammed her in the chair. Loco grabbed a cord and put it around her neck and choked her. I waited until the bitch looked like she was about to pass out again, before signaling Loco to let her go. She sat in the chair trembling, and holding her arm, gasping for air.

Esteban cracked his knuckles and stood over top of her, looking at Loco. Loco was staring back at Esteban with an evil grin on his face. It was as if they were having a silent conversation. Loco pulled the cord again, choking, as Esteban punched her a few times in the face. The bitch was leaking from her nose and mouth. Gael started laughing. *These some twisted ass niggas,* I thought, as I looked at the pleasure that was displayed on the three of their faces.

I grabbed her purse off the table as I walked over to her, digging in it for her phone. I placed my foot in the chair between her legs and leaned down.

"Call Alexia," I instructed as I passed her the phone. "Try something funny and I'll shoot your hand off," I warned her, placing my gun on her hand.

With trembling hands, she scrolled through her contacts. She hit the call button and I hit the speaker button. The phone was ringing but she didn't answer. Ashley sat in the chair bouncing her knee, begging Alexia to answer the phone. Her voicemail came on. I ordered her to keep calling back to back until she answered.

"What the hell do you want?" she answered in frustration.

"Hello, Raquel," I spoke in a calm but frightening voice.

She was silent.

"Alexia, I know you're there, please answer," Ashley pleaded.

"What, Adonis?" she snapped.

"I want my daughter and I want her NOW," I demanded.

"Fuck you, Adonis, I wanted my child too," she spat into the phone.

Loco choked Ashley again, then let her go.

"Pllllease, Alexia, give him his child. Where are you?" Ashley cried as she pleaded to her sister.

"You hear the pain your sister is in? GIVE ME BACK MY CHILD OR I'LL MAKE HER SUFFER!" I yelled.

"Ashley never gave a fuck about me. She only helped me to get her son Havoc in the game. Fuck her," she chuckled.

"That's not true, Alexia, I love you," Ashley whined.

"FUCK ALL THIS SHIT!" I shouted. "I don't give a fuck about you or yo' got damn sister. I want my daughter. If you don't agree to meet me with her, I'll blow you sister's got damn head off right now," I threatened.

"I don't give a fuck. Kill the bitch. I already killed Serene." The line went dead.

I felt my heart sink to my feet as raged filled my body.

"YOU FUCKIN" BITCH!" I screamed and started raining blows down on Ashley. She was screaming in agony.

I saw red. I grabbed the bitch out of the chair and slung her to the ground like a rag doll. I wrapped my hands around her throat and started choking her. I watched while her swollen bruised face started turning red. She was scratching at my hands, tryna push me off of her. I just squeezed tighter and tighter. I could hear her bones cracking but that still wasn't enough. I snapped her neck but I still couldn't let her go.

"Adonis, she's gone, man." Loco was tryna pull me off of her but I couldn't let that bitch go.

All I kept hearing was Alexia saying she killed my baby. I wanted to kill this bitch over and over again. Esteban and Gael pulled me off the bitch. I was still dragging her lifeless body with me.

Finally, I dropped the bitch and my pain came to surface. I let out a loud thunderous roar, and started punching holes in the wall.

"ADONIS!" Loco screamed, tryna get my attention.

I wasn't hearing nothing. Alexia's words were the only thing I could hear. I couldn't get any type of satisfaction. I just wanted to destroy anything in my path. Loco grabbed me and tackled me to the ground.

"Look, nigga, stop that shit. We all about to go down. Call the cleaning crew and let's get the fuck outta here." My chest hurt and I felt like I couldn't catch my breath.

"Come on man, get up," he spoke in a low voice.

I ran my hands over my face and took a few deep breaths, tryna get myself under control. Loco was right. If I didn't get it together, we were all gonna go down. I pulled out my phone and called Roland.

***

The plane ride was silent; I was wondering how was I going to tell Venus that our baby is dead. She's not going to be able to handle that. I have to find this bitch if it's the last thing I do on this earth. I ran my hands over my face and let out a sigh. I felt numb.

"Here, man, have a drink." Gael passed me a glass.

I drunk it down in one gulp then poured another. Loco came and sat down across from me with a glass. I could see the sadness in his eyes as he opened and closed his mouth. He looked like he wanted to say something, but truthfully what can you say?

We arrived at the Reagan National. I told Loco and the rest to leave me so I could speak to

Rojas alone. I felt a lump growing in my throat as I pictured my baby in my head. I only got to hold her for a little while, feel her heart next to mine. Smell her scent as I snuggled her against my cheek. A lone tear fell down my face. I laid my head back and closed my eyes.

"Adonis, I'm so sorry," I heard Rojas's voice as he entered the plane.

I wiped the tears from my eyes as I sat up.

"Thank you, Rojas," I said in a low voice.

"If there's anything I can do, call me," he insisted.

"Our business is done, Rojas," I told him as I passed him the briefcase containing the money I was giving him for the use of his plane.

"Keep it," he stated, sliding the briefcase back to me. "It was a pleasure doing business with you, Adonis. Keep in touch." I nodded as I stood to shake his hand.

I walked off the plane and got in my car.

"We gon' get through this, Adonis," Loco assured me, giving me a brotherly hug.

I started up the car and pulled out of the airport, dreading the fact that I have to go home and tell Venus that I'm responsible for our child's death. She's never gonna forgive me. I picked up the phone to call her. I needed to hear her voice.

Venus

Adonis was calling my phone as I was turning the corner to our street.

"Hey, babe, when you coming home?" I answered.

"I just stepped off the plane, I'm in the car heading home now," he replied. He sounded a little off.

"What's wrong?" I asked. He was silent for a few seconds.

"Nothing, I'll talk to you when I get home. I'm on the way now," he replied.

I had a feeling that something was wrong. I know he wasn't gonna tell me until he got home. I told him I would see him soon.

I pulled in the driveway and turned the car off. Harmony was in the back seat half asleep. I unhooked her and told her to hurry in the house so she could get a bath before she falls asleep. She started whining for me to pick her up. I picked her up and headed to the door.

"Girl, you getting too big for mommy to carry you," I said, kissing her on the side of her head. She giggled.

I put her down so I could open the door. I noticed that the alarm didn't beep. *Damn, I forgot to put the alarm on again, Adonis would've had a fit,* I thought. I closed and locked the door and activated the alarm.

"Harmony, go get ready for bed and a bath," I instructed.

She took off running up the steps and I went to put Adonis's food on the stove. I started going up the steps and went to her room. She wasn't there.

"Harmony," I called out, but she didn't answer.

I went into the bathroom and she wasn't in there either. I called her name again. Still no answer.

My heart started pounding and fear grew inside of me. I rushed out the bathroom and was on my way to my room, when I heard Harmony's laughter coming out of Serene's room. I was confused. *What was she doing in the baby's room?* I asked myself.

I went up to the door and listened to see if I could hear her doing anything. It was silent, then I heard her giggle again. I opened the door. My heart stopped. Raquel was sitting in the rocking chair with Harmony on her lap, reading a book and stroking her hair. Her hand was in her pocket as if she had a gun pointed at Harmony's back.

"What are you two doing in here?" I asked in a pleasant sounding voice as I walked into the room.

I had to keep my composure so I didn't alarm Harmony.

"I was just reading little Harmony here a story," she replied in a silvery voice. "Harmony, why don't you show your mommy the picture I gave you." She peered at me with a half-smile. Harmony hopped off her lap and ran over to me.

"Look, Mommy. Raquel had a little baby girl like you," she beamed, passing me the picture.

A nervous feeling washed over me and my hands trembled, taking the picture out of her hand. My heart stopped beating as I stared at the picture of my beautiful amber eyed baby girl.

"She's adorable, isn't she? She looks just like her daddy," she taunted.

I held my breath, fighting back the tears I felt forming in my throat.

"Come here, Harmony," Raquel commanded, motioning her to stand by her side.

I refused to allow Harmony to go back over to that crazy bitch. I didn't know what Raquel was capable of. I exhaled the breath I was holding and regained my composure. Raquel called for her again.

Before Harmony could move, I grabbed her by her shoulders.

"We gonna play a game now honey, it's called three claps. You go and hide and I have to come and find you, ok?" I spoke in a cheerful tone as I squatted down. She nodded.

"I'm playing too," Raquel snickered.

"Listen to me, Harmony. You have to hide where nobody can see or hear you. Hide really good and mommy will call out the first clap. I want you to clap so that mommy can try to find you, ok?" She nodded.

I hugged her and whispered in her ear, "Don't come out until you hear me say I need my chocolate kiss."

I kissed her cheek. "Now, I'm gonna count, you go hide. Remember what I told you," I instructed. "One...two..." I started counting and she took off running down the steps.

I continued counting as Raquel picked up Serene's bear and snuggled it.

"First clap, Harmony!" I yelled. I heard a faint clap in a distance. I knew she was far away. "Where's my baby, Raquel?" I asked.

She pointed her gun on me. "My name is Alexia. Didn't hubby tell you?" she raised her eyebrows. "He's in Detroit right now looking for me, but I'm not there, am I?" she chuckled. It wasn't a normal, cheerful chuckle; it was more sinister sounding.

"Raquel—" I started.

"BITCH, MY NAME IS ALEXIA," she shouted, cutting me off.

She came towards me with the gun aimed at my head.

"You just couldn't leave him alone, could you? Me and Adonis were happy, but you had to keep throwing yourself at him. You selfish ass bitch." She slapped me in the face with the gun.

My head hit the dresser as I went crashing to the floor. I was disoriented as I struggled to pull myself up. Alexia used her foot to push me back down on the floor. She kneeled down beside me, grabbed me by the hair, and lifted my head up.

"You a weak bitch. You and your husband took my life away. I lost my baby when he killed Maurice, so I took yours." She leaned in closer and said, "I killed your precious Serene, and Harmony is next." Hearing her say that she killed my baby tore my heart in to pieces.

She banged my head on the floor and started walking towards the room door, then she paused.

"Second clap, Harmony," she yelled, looking at me with an evil smirk.

I heard Harmony's faint clap. Alexia snickered then continued out the door. I don't know if it was fear or anger, but I felt a fire burn through my body. I was not letting that bitch find my daughter. With every ounce of strength I had in my body, I got off of the floor and charged at her. I tackled her by her waist, sending her crashing to the ground, knocking the gun out of her hand. We both were on the floor, wrestling and fighting. I punched her in the face, knocking her off of me. I straddled her.

"YOU KILLED MY BABY, YOU FUCKIN' BITCH!" I had a handful of her hair in both hands, banging her head on the floor with every word.

I continued banging her head over and over until I saw blood seeping out of the back of her head. She was dazed. I got off of her and grabbed the gun. I heard the alarm deactivate.

POW! POW!

Adonis

The sound of gunshots echoed through the hall as I walked through the door. I pulled my gun out, cocked it, then ran up the steps. Loco was right behind me, ready to kill. I almost reached the top of the steps.

POW!

A bullet ricocheted off the rail and the wall above my head.

"Venus, put the gun down, it's me," I said as I lowered my gun.

"I know it's you. You did this, you killed my baby. I warned you," she cried as she stood up, pointing the gun at me.

POW!

She shot at me again, hitting the wall instead. Thank God she didn't know how to aim or my ass would have been dead.

"Venus, listen to me. Put the gun down, you don't want to do this," I tried to reason with her.

I slowly stepped on the top step. Alexia's lifeless body was lying on the floor beside Venus with a pool of blood around her.

"You lied to me, you knew she had my baby," she said angrily, as she pulled the trigger on the gun again.

The gun jammed. As she fidgeted with the gun, I rushed toward her and snatched it out of her hand. She started swinging, punching me in my chest and crying.

"I hate you. I hate you," she repeated as tears poured from her eyes.

I wrapped my arms around her, holding her tightly, as she struggled to free herself from my grip. She gave up fighting and let her head sink into my chest, before she broke down crying. Her trembling body went limp in my arms. I picked her up and carried her into the room. I sat her down on the bed and held her as she continued weeping. She was broken.

"Y'all alright?" Loco asked from the doorway.

"Yeah, we good," I replied.

I was hesitant to release the hold I had on Venus to make sure she wasn't physically hurt. She just tried to shoot my ass. I couldn't believe that shit. Once she was calm, I let her go. I noticed a lump on her forehead. I touched it and she winced in pain.

"Loco, go get some ice," I demanded. He hurried down the steps.

"Where's Harmony?" I asked wiping tears from her eyes.

Her eyes grew big as if she remembered. She held on to me as she stood up and walked out into the hallway.

"Third clap, Harmony!" she yelled.

I was confused. What the hell is third clap? I wondered.

"Third clap, Harmony!" she yelled louder.

We still didn't hear anything. Venus grabbed on to the wall and the rail and started going down the steps.

"Hold on." I grabbed on to her and helped her down the steps.

"I need my chocolate kiss!" she yelled.

"Venus, what the fuck are you doing?" I asked, still confused.

"I told her we were playing the game three claps, and not to come out until I say I need my chocolate kiss," she explained. "Oh my God, where is she?" she asked as tears filled her eyes.

I sat her on the sofa and gave her the ice bag Loco made and told her to put that on her head.

"Where do you think she was hiding?" I asked.

"She had to be somewhere down here because her clap was distant," she replied.

"We'll find her," I stated as me and Loco started searching the entire downstairs area.

"I'll check the basement," Loco said as he rushed down the steps.

I started checking the counters in the kitchen.

"I got her," Loco yelled from the basement.

We heard Harmony's little giggle and Venus burst into tears. Loco emerged from the basement with Harmony in his arms.

"Mommy, I was a good hider; you didn't find me," she chuckled as he passed her to Venus.

"She was asleep in the closet of her playroom," Loco informed us.

"You did a good job hiding," Venus said as she hugged her tightly.

"Yeah, you did," I stated as I kissed her on the top of her head.

My phone started ringing in my pocket. It was smoke.

"What's up?" I answered.

"Those other niggas Lavelle used is on the way," he replied.

I didn't know what the hell Smoke was talking about. But Loco told me he called Smoke to get a cleaning crew since my crew wasn't back from Detroit yet. I really didn't give a damn who came. I just wanted this damn mess cleaned up quickly. I told Venus to take Harmony to the basement lie her in the guest bed while we clean up the mess. She got up and started walking towards the basement. I grabbed her by the arm to stop her.

"I'm sorry. I know that ain't enough, but that's all I can say right now," I said.

She shook her head then turned around and walked away.

I flopped down on the sofa and covered my face with my hands. I let out a loud sigh. I felt something cold tap my arm. I looked up.

"You need this," Loco said, passing me a drink.

He sat in the chair across from me with a drink in his hand.

"Yo' ass better sleep with one eye open tonight." He shook his head.

"Fuck that, I ain't ever sleeping. She real live tried to shoot me," I stated in disbelief.

"Yeah, man, that shit was crazy as hell," Loco avowed.

We were both at a loss for words. A few minutes later, the cleaning crew was there. Loco gave them their instructions and they went upstairs.

Venus came upstairs.

"Harmony asleep?" I asked.

"I want you out," she spoke calmly.

"Venus, I'm not leaving tonight or any other night. Go downstairs with Harmony and we can talk later." She looked at me with narrowed eyes, she snickered, then headed back down the steps.

"Nigga, you straight?" Loco asked with a twisted up face.

"Yeah, we got some shit to get through but we'll be ok," I replied reaching for my ringing phone.

"Muthafucka, she just tried to shoot yo' ass. Did you forget?" I heard his question but I didn't answer. I was looking at my phone wondering what the fuck Whitman was calling me for.

"Yeah," I answered.

"You home?" he asked.

"Yeah, why?" I questioned with a perplexed look.

"I received a call tonight, and I have something that belongs to you. I'm on the way to see you in five." The line went dead.

What the fuck was that shit about? I thought.

Loco noticed the baffled look on my face and asked what was going on. I shrugged my shoulders. I really didn't know what that strange call was about. The cleaning crew came downstairs carrying a tub containing Alexia's body.

"We gonna take this to the spot and take care of this. Everything else is done." I thanked him and walked them to the door.

"Aight, nigga. I'ma chill out to see what the fuck Whitman talkin' about in case some shit needs to be handled, then I'm going home to my lady," Loco said as he poured us another round of drinks.

I laid my head back on the sofa thinking about Venus and wondering what exactly went down tonight. I shook my head. *This has been a long and fucked up ass day*, I thought. I closed my eyes and started praying that Whitman wasn't about to come to me with some bullshit. I swear if some more fucked up shit happens tonight, I'm gonna snap.

A few minutes later, Whitman called and told me to meet him outside. Me and Loco went to the door and opened it. Whitman and Dumas were both standing there. Whitman was holding a baby wrapped in a pink blanket.

"Pastor Rogers called me and told me he found a baby in front of his church," he informed me.

I stood frozen. My heart was pounding so hard, I felt like it was gonna jump out of my chest. It couldn't be Serene. Alexia said she killed her. I didn't know what to feel. I was happy that my little angel was home safe and sound, but at the same time, I wasn't sure if it was mine.

"Adonis, it's Serene," Whitman assured me, as he moved the blanket from her face.

As soon as I saw her chubby little face, it was real. Serene was home. I exhaled a breath of relief as I reached for my baby. Tears filled my eyes when I snuggled her against my chest. I was holding my daughter and I didn't want to let her go. I covered her back up.

"VENUS, COME QUICK!" I shouted down the steps.

"What the hell do you want Adonis?" she fumed as she stomped up the steps.

She rounded the corner. I was standing in the living room holding our daughter.

"She didn't kill her, Venus. Serene, she's alive," I said in a brittle voice.

She stood frozen with wide eyes and her hand covering her mouth. Her chest was rising and falling rapidly as she was trying to catch her breath. With tears filling her eyes, she slowly walked over to me. I kissed Serene's forehead over her blanket.

"Meet our daughter," I stated, passing Serene to Venus.

Venus

My hands were shaking as I took Serene in my arms. Was this real? Was I going to wake up without her again, like I had done before so many nights? I don't think I can bear another night without my daughter. The sweet muffled sounds of her coos of contentment vibrated from the pink cashmere blanket that she was wrapped in. The soft scent of orchids, and natural baby touched my nose. I rocked her gently.

"Baby, are you ok?" Adonis asked softly, his voice going unnoticed.

I gently pulled back the blanket, and a pair of identical amber eyes captured mine. I was lost. It was her! I was holding the baby that I missed so much in my arms. I pulled her so close, her soft honey complexion could've melted into mine.

"I love you, Serene. I missed you so much!" I cried into the blanket.

My baby girl… my world was made whole again. I looked up at Adonis and saw my husband, father of my child, and the love of my life. Not the man that I wanted to hurt hours ago, but the man I knew he was inside. He had gone through hell and hot water to get our princess back. Adonis leaned and kissed Serene, then me.

"I finally have my world back," he said in a softly spoken voice as he gently stroked Serene's cheek.

"You still want me?" he asked. I nodded.

"Good 'cause I wasn't going anywhere. You stuck with me and all my bullshit for the rest of your life. I love you, Venus," he replied.

Looking in to his loving eyes, I couldn't deny it. We were made for each other.

"I love you too, Adonis," I said in a softly spoken voice.

I pulled Serene close again, almost as if she would disappear.

"Welcome home, sweetheart."

Epilogue

A year later

Kay Kay

Venus, Layna, Ms. Bowman, and my mother, Jailin Turner, were in the room helping me get dressed. It was my wedding day, and I was nervous as hell. I kept sweating and fidgeting around, misplacing shit.

"Is everything set up outside? You think I need to go check?" I inquired.

Me and Loco decided to have an outdoor wedding since we both loved nature. Our backyard was huge, and he had it renovated into a beautiful oasis, kind of like the one I saw on this show on

HGTV. I thought it was the perfect scenery for our small wedding.

"Girl, calm yo' ass down! You know everything is going to be fine," my mother said, wiping the beads of sweat from my brows.

"You're right, ma. I need to get myself together," I admitted, turning the fan on. I felt like it was 100 degrees. "I really love Loco, so I don't know why I'm so fuckin' nervous," I added.

"Girl, 'cause you scared his ass gon' get cold feet," Ms. Bowman chuckled.

They all started laughing.

"Girl, Loco probably in that room nervous as hell too," Venus stated. She walked over to me and gave me a hug. "Loco loves you, Kay Kay, everything is gonna be ok," she assured me.

"Y'all right. I just have to calm down and get dressed." Ejoma shook her head as she started fixing my hair and makeup.

When she was finished, Venus helped me into my dress.

"Bitch, did you have to get a mermaid style dress with all that ass?" Venus asked jokingly.

I turned around and checked my ass out in the mirror.

"Loco gonna go crazy when he sees me in this. You know he loves my ass," I said, wiggling my hips.

I turned back around and saw how beautiful I looked. I loved how the silver and crystal trimming ran up the front side of the dress, but what I loved mostly was the way it stood out against the white.

"Girl, Venus, you designed the fuck outta this dress," I marveled.

"It is the perfect dress; you did a great job," my mother agreed, walking over to me.

She fluffed out the silver and white chiffon tiers that went around the bottom of the dress.

Venus placed my head piece on the top of my head. The light bounced off of the crystals, making them simmer.

"Now, the finishing touches," my mother said, walking over to me with a box in her hand.

"I wore this on my wedding day, and your grandmother wore this on hers too." She opened the box revealing an exquisite diamond necklace.

"This is stunning," I choked, tryna fight the lump that formed in my throat.

I turned around so she could place the necklace on my neck. It was the perfect piece to add to my strapless dress.

"You look like royalty," Venus complimented as tears filled her eyes.

I glanced at myself in the mirror one more time "I do," I said in a low voice.

"You are a beautiful bride," Ms. Bowman said, kissing me on the cheek.

"Thank you," I smiled.

My father, Kentlee Turner, knocked on the door. My mother let him in.

"My God, you look absolutely amazing," he said, grinning proudly.

Even though my parents are divorced, my father remained a huge part of my life, and I loved him for that.

"Thanks, Dad, for walking me down the aisle. It means a lot to me."

"Kaylee, I wouldn't have it any other way. I know I didn't like Loco at first. He was your typical street nigga, but I see that he's good for you, and he loves you. That's all that matters." He kissed me on the cheek. Then he turned to my mother and told her that she looked beautiful as well and kissed her on the cheek.

"You know you always look handsome," she flirted. I shook my head.

My father looked in the mirror and straightened his jacket.

"You right, Jailin, I am a handsome ass dude. You shouldn't have divorced me," he snickered.

"You should have kept your dick in your pants," she gibed with her hand on her hip.

"Ok you two. It's my wedding, don't start bickering," I chided.

"You know I love that woman," he expressed, blowing her a kiss. She shook her head and rolled her eyes, but she was blushing.

My father walked over to me. "You ready?" he asked.

"I am," I beamed.

Loco

Standing under the floral arch looking around my yard at all the decorations, made this day a reality for me. I never thought I would actually do this getting married shit, but Kay Kay changed that. She changed a lot for me. I used to talk shit to Adonis about being tied down with Venus. Now I'm standing at the altar getting prepared to marry my queen.

"I'm clownin' right now, nigga. I thought we wasn't gon' see yo' ass tying no fuckin' knot no time soon, muthafucka," Adonis chuckled, as he came to stand by my side as my best man.

"Man, fuck you. I'm still not tied down like yo' ass," I replied, giving him dap.

"Shiiiid, nigga, Kay Kay got yo' ass locked all the way the fuck down," he laughed.

"You got jokes. Kay Kay knows who wear the pants in my fuckin' house," I replied.

"I don't know, nigga. Kay Kay rocks the hell outta a pair of True's," he smirked.

"Fuck you, nigga. Venus's lil' ass got an iron fist. She'll knock yo' ass out," I teased.

"And Kay Kay don't? You threatened her life several times and her ass still don't give a fuck 'bout shit you talkin', nigga, fuck you talkin' 'bout?" he laughed.

Before I could respond, the preacher walked up to the podium and announced that the ceremony was about to begin. All the chatter stopped. The music started and Harmony walked down the aisle holding Orlando's and Serene's hands.

Seeing my son come down the aisle with Serene made a nigga get all choked up and shit. He looked just like me: tall, dark and handsome. He even has little dreads and all. I glanced at Serene and thought about all the shit we went through to get her back, seeing her walking down the aisle was a blessing.

"You straight, nigga?" Adonis whispered, leaning in so only I could hear him.

"Yeah, I'm good, just loving the moment," I admitted.

"Yo, Kay Kay got yo' ass soft as shit now," he chuckled lightly.

"Don't get it twisted, nigga. I'm still down for the murda," I replied.

Even though we gave up the street life and just run the clubs, I'm still the same crazy ass muthafucka as I was before. Difference is I have a family to worry about now, and they come first.

"Man, lil' O is yo' twin for real," he said.

"Yeah, I know," I shook my head. "It's funny how that lil' nigga changed my life. Shit nigga, you talkin', both of yo' girls look like you. But lil AJ, his lil' ass looks exactly like Venus," I avowed.

Venus's fertile ass got pregnant right after Serene came home and her and Adonis made up.

"I know, his lil momma's boy ass... I got to break that shit," he chuckled.

"Man, I'm glad you and Venus were able to work that shit out," I spoke truthfully.

"Me too, man. She hated my ass for a while, but we pulled through. We were made for each other, just like you and Kay Kay," he replied, staring at Venus walking down the aisle.

Everyone gasped as Kay Kay stood under the floral archway, waiting for her cue to start walking in. The organ player started playing "All My Life" by K-Ci and Jo-Jo, and the singer started singing the lyrics. Kay Kay marched down the aisle with the biggest smile on her face. I couldn't take my eyes off of her. She looked fuckin' gorgeous as hell. Her sexy ass had a nigga ready to skip the ceremony and go straight to the honeymoon. Her plump, juicy ass was definitely getting my attention. She had that ass sitting out there like it was waiting for me to go balls deep in it.

The preacher started the ceremony and I couldn't wait for him to tell me that I could kiss my wife. Standing at the alter hand in hand, staring into those beautiful eyes, made me fall in love with her all over again.

It was time for the vows. Of course, it was her idea to write our own. She changed the shit outta me. Who would have thought that I would be marrying a bitch, now writing my own vows talking about feelings and shit? I kept it short, simple, and straight to the point.

"Kaylee, I love you and I promise to be faithful, to provide for you, protect you, always be truthful, and to love you for life, and treat you like the queen that you are."

"Orlando, my king. I promise to love you, be faithful to you, trust you, to always be honest, let you lead me, and to always be your best friend, and your rider, and to love you forever." I was glad she kept hers short, simple, and straight to the point, just like me. That's why we fit, we think as one.

The preacher finally pronounced us man and wife. I kissed my wife for the first time, and it was the best kiss we ever shared.

"Did I tell you how fuckin' beautiful you look?" I asked my wife, sitting at the table at our reception, watching everyone dancing and having fun.

"Yeah, but you can tell me again," she replied, smiling. "Oh, you look so handsome; I can't wait to get to our hotel," she smirked. "Shit, this our house, we can just sneak away." She licked her lips.

"That's why I married yo' freaky ass. You think just like me." I stood up and grabbed her hand.

"You are the most beautiful bride I have ever seen. I was proud watching yo' sexy ass walking down the aisle to be my wife," I boasted as I kissed her hand.

She smiled and said, "I was proud knowing that I was going to be standing beside the most handsome man in the world for the rest of my life. I'm honored to be your wife." I kissed her again.

"Oh my goodness, are you two ever gonna stop kissing? And where the hell y'all sneaking off to?" We both gave her a *you already know* look. "Freaks." We laughed as she walked off, shaking her head.

"Well, Mrs. Gaines, what's next in our future?" I asked as we started walking towards the house.

"I don't know, Mr. Gaines, but as long as I'm with you, I know I can just sit back and enjoy the ride." I kissed her.

The sound of Harmony's distinctive little giggle caught our attention. We stopped and looked in the direction where it was coming from. Harmony was sitting on Adonis's lap as they all watched Serene dance with Lil' O. Adonis had his arm around Venus as she cradled AJ in her arms, looking like the perfect little family.

"They look so happy," Kay Kay boasted as she stared at them.

"Yeah, they do. I want to have more kids, and have what they have one day," I said, placing my arms around Kay Kay's waist.

"Me too," she admitted. "I want to have a perfectly, imperfect little family like Adonis and Venus."

The End

Interested in becoming a part of the

Treasured Publications family?

Submit manuscripts to

Info@Treasuredpub.com

Like us on Facebook:

Treasured Publications

Be sure to text **Treasured** to **22828**

To subscribe to our Mailing List.

Never miss a release or contest again!

CPSIA information can be obtained
at www.ICGtesting.com
Printed in the USA
LVOW04s0046251016
510071LV00013B/199/P